MW01505846

Mia drew ~~~ headed into Sante's office—leaving his door wide open behind her.

Trying to steady her heartbeat. The appalling thing was that increasingly her body responded with chaos to his proximity. It didn't seem to care that he was a heartless jerk who'd betrayed her brother, her body just wanted his near. So she was ignoring her body. Controlling it.

"You've screwed up my scheduling." He glared at her.

"Where?"

He jabbed a finger at the screen and she was forced to round his desk to study it. Big mistake. There was nowhere near enough of a barrier between them and she desperately needed to calm her overexcited response.

"You've blocked out a significant portion of my day tomorrow."

She leaned closer and he turned his head toward her, meaning his mouth was only inches from hers. It was *searingly* intimate. It would take nothing to lower hers and—

What the hell was she thinking? Why had the idea to kiss him popped into her head? She stared into his brown eyes for three seconds too long.

A brand-new, spicy duet from Harlequin Presents authors Natalie Anderson and Heidi Rice!

Enemy Tycoons

Sante Trovato and Dario Lorenti's friendship began in an English boarding school, bonded by their Italian heritage—despite their vastly different backgrounds. Until a tragic accident and a deep betrayal tore their bond apart, causing their once-unshakeable friendship to go up in flames, and turning them into bitter enemies...

Years later, the lives of the powerful tech tycoons intersect once again!

Enemies Until After Hours by Natalie Anderson

Tech billionaire Sante is appalled to find his new temporary assistant is his enemy's sister, Mia. But Sante is her boss, so their scorching, *forbidden* attraction must be contained. Until a storm leaves them stranded together, and the desire they've been denying suddenly ignites!

Available now!

And don't miss Dario and Tali's story

Boss's Bride Price by Heidi Rice

Ruthless tycoon Dario will do anything to secure his inheritance—even propose a marriage of convenience to the spirited estate manager, Tali, who he was just about to fire! As they head to Sicily for his sister's wedding, Dario's intent on unleashing Tali's long suppressed sexuality. So long as no emotions get involved...

Coming soon!

ENEMIES UNTIL AFTER HOURS

NATALIE ANDERSON

Harlequin

PRESENTS

If you purchased this book without a cover you should be aware that this book is stolen property. It was reported as "unsold and destroyed" to the publisher, and neither the author nor the publisher has received any payment for this "stripped book."

MIX
Paper | Supporting responsible forestry
FSC® C021394
www.fsc.org

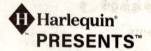

Harlequin®
PRESENTS™

Recycling programs for this product may not exist in your area.

ISBN-13: 978-1-335-21363-1

Enemies Until After Hours

Copyright © 2026 by Natalie Anderson

All rights reserved. No part of this book may be used or reproduced in any manner whatsoever without written permission.

Without limiting the exclusive rights of any author, contributor or the publisher of this publication, any unauthorized use of this publication to train generative artificial intelligence (AI) technologies is expressly prohibited. Harlequin also exercises their rights under Article 4(3) of the Digital Single Market Directive 2019/790 and expressly reserves this publication from the text and data mining exception.

This is a work of fiction. Names, characters, places and incidents are either the product of the author's imagination or are used fictitiously. Any resemblance to actual persons, living or dead, businesses, companies, events or locales is entirely coincidental.

For questions and comments about the quality of this book, please contact us at CustomerService@Harlequin.com.

TM and ® are trademarks of Harlequin Enterprises ULC.

Harlequin Enterprises ULC
22 Adelaide St. West, 41st Floor
Toronto, Ontario M5H 4E3, Canada
www.Harlequin.com

HarperCollins Publishers
Macken House, 39/40 Mayor Street Upper,
Dublin 1, D01 C9W8, Ireland
www.HarperCollins.com

Printed in Lithuania

USA TODAY bestselling author **Natalie Anderson** writes emotional contemporary romance full of sparkling banter, sizzling heat and uplifting endings—perfect for readers who love to escape with empowered heroines and arrogant alphas who are too sexy for their own good. When she's not writing, you'll find Natalie wrangling her four children, three cats, two goldfish and one dog...and snuggled in a heap on the sofa with her husband at the end of the day. Follow her at natalie-anderson.com.

Books by Natalie Anderson

Harlequin Presents

The Boss's Stolen Bride
My One-Night Heir

Billion-Dollar Christmas Confessions

Carrying Her Boss's Christmas Baby

Innocent Royal Runaways

Impossible Heir for the King
Back to Claim His Crown

Billion-Dollar Bet

Billion-Dollar Dating Game

Convenient Wives Club

Their Altar Arrangement
Boss's Baby Acquisition
Greek Vows Revisited

Visit the Author Profile page
at Harlequin.com for more titles.

For Deb

CHAPTER ONE

MIA SIMONINI GLIDED along the polished wooden floors of the gleaming office, humming her favourite song. First to arrive, last to leave; that was her mantra and she was killing it. Admittedly, for most of the ten days she'd been working here, the office had been more than half-empty so maybe that wasn't that much of a claim, but she had a plan to tempt the creative and coding geniuses to come and work in person for at least a few more hours each week. Small things could have big impacts—not that Mia herself was small. Nor quiet. But as she was alone right now, the latter didn't matter and the former never had. She bit into her cannoncino, savouring the silky rich cream and the light, flaky pastry, and her hum became a guttural moan of gastronomic delight. The thing was sheer buttery joy. She'd discovered the best pastry shop in Rome, and calling in her order on her way to work was her reward for these early starts and diligence. She set her coffee on her desk but as she took another bite of pastry, a dollop of cream plopped onto her shirt.

'Damn.'

Not *quite* killing it. But if it weren't for her boobs the cream would have landed on her keyboard, so there was a marginal silver lining to the snafu. Mia never had mastered the art of sitting down to eat tiny portions slowly—'like a lady'—as her jerk of a father had frequently harangued her to. He'd not liked her appetite. Nor her enthusiasm. Honestly, not anything much about her. But he was no longer around and Mia didn't know why she allowed his judgy words to echo within her still.

Get it together.

Mia was used to jobs where having some food on her clothing was an occupational hazard and thus if not quite acceptable, then at least understandable, but this gig wasn't one of them. She was temporary office manager for a tech start-up incubator that clearly had too much money to throw about, given the luxury refurbishment of the historic building in central Rome where it was housed—and the fact that half the staff never bothered to show up to use it. Including the boss. She'd had doubts about taking on this contract for her dear friend Adele; tech was not her sector—truth be told, she barely understood what some of those apps did—but she hoped that managing a bunch of genius programmers wasn't unlike managing any other bunch of strong-minded individuals. Because Adele had been desperate. She'd needed immediate cover so she could care for her husband, who'd suffered a serious medical event, and as luck would have it, Mia had opted to pass on her next cruise ship contract and so was able to step in. It was a weird set-up, though—gleaming and new and clearly successful...just run by ghosts. Though at this moment, the staff all being absent was a good thing. Mia snatched her spare top—it was hardly the first time she'd spilled food on herself so she kept one at work—and nipped into the private bathroom in the CEO's suite as it was nearest. Of all the

AWOL staff, he was the one who was never there. But she needed to move because the stalwarts who did show up daily—company lawyer Paolo and his property team, plus the chief financial officer Carla and her two investment analysts—would arrive any second.

With her fresh shirt wedged in the crook of her arm and the remaining pastry held between her teeth, Mia unbuttoned her blouse, still humming her tune of the day as she walked through the empty office to the bathroom and turned to the mirror.

'Who are you?'

She whirled, the two halves of her cream-smeared blouse splaying wide with the speed of her spin. She stared, utterly unable to answer and not because of the pastry hanging from her mouth like an oversize cigar. Sweet mother of mercy. There was a man already in the bathroom.

Not just any man. He was about as bare chested as she—while his shirt was on his arms and shoulders he was still in the process of buttoning it up, which meant she saw flexing pecs and washboard abs and a seemingly endless expanse of lean, bronzed skin and a light smattering of dark hair that arrowed down into tailored dark grey suit trousers that emphasised his narrow hips and long legs and—

'Who are you?' he repeated in rapid Italian.

Who was she? Who was *he*? Mia froze on the outside and melted on the inside. He was tall, dark and very much looking like he'd just stepped out of the shower. The scent of soap tantalised her suddenly suffocating lungs. The single trickle of water slipping its way down his finely muscled torso was too fascinating and she snapped her attention up to his face.

Oh. Oh *my*. He'd freshly shaved and that simply high-lighted his sculpted cheekbones and square jawline that screamed to be touched while his hair was slightly too long and too unruly for the pristine carved perfection of the rest of him.

Good Lord, the man was gorgeous.

Her brain refused to compute. At all. But there was something familiar about those bottomless, dreamy brown eyes. Was it possible that she knew him? Was it possible her brain would ever work again?

She removed the end of the cannoncino from her mouth and quickly licked her lip, certain there'd be an errant flake of pastry; there always was. Too late, she realised her struggle to breathe was because of the lingering steam in the air. He'd definitely showered in here. And *that* meant—

'You're the boss,' she muttered.

The guy who'd been absent for over a week. The one her friend Adele adored and wanted Mia to protect and do everything for without question.

'Who are you and why are you here?' He switched to English immediately.

So much for thinking her Italian had improved. She'd lost most of her first language when her mother had died and she'd had to go live with her father in England, but she'd been working on it and—

'Are you the cleaner?' he prompted, his gaze grazing down her body.

She grabbed her blouse with her spare hand, but there was a lot of Mia to cover. A polite man would avert his eyes. This man was not polite. This man took his time to scrutinise every inch of her exposed skin, and given his forbidding expression he was not impressed. He could not stand more ramrod straight. Or still. Or look more grumpy.

'Did one of the coders hire you as some kind of inappropriate entertainment?' he growled.

OMG—had he just mistaken her for an exotic dancer? *At seven o'clock on a Monday morning?*

Mia straightened as best she could given the gaping blouse issues, determined to recover some dignity. 'I was hired by Adele.'

'What?' He cocked his head and stepped closer. 'Why? When?' His bottomless soulful gaze turned icy. 'To do *what*?'

Mia didn't answer. He still looked disturbingly *familiar* and if only she could get her brain to work, she might rake up why. But surely, she would remember if she'd ever met a man this ridiculously hot?

'Who are you?' He took another step closer and his voice dropped to sub-zero temperatures—perfectly matching his frigid glare.

Mia was used to far worse than disapproving looks and quelling glances and being told to be quiet because once again she was being too much. This jerk's supercilious ability to look down his nose at her was nothing on the acid that streamed from her father's tongue. This ass and his not-so-silent distaste could take a hike.

She stared back at him. Hard. And shoved the remainder of the pastry into her mouth. It wasn't the first time she'd stuffed in food to stop herself saying something she shouldn't, but it was the most stupid.

Because suddenly she placed his face. More precisely, his *eyes*. She finally remembered those meltingly deep brown eyes. And now she didn't want to answer any of his questions. Now she needed a moment to recover.

Adele had referred to her boss only as Santo—Saint. Mia had figured it was some kind of inside joke given Santo Antonio was the name of the software company. Mia had gotten full access to Adele's email, and her boss had only his first initial on the email address and he signed off with simply an S.

She'd had only a day and a half with Adele in a frantic handover before the older woman had needed to get back to the hospital. Mia had listened and not questioned anything unless it had been essential because Adele was already struggling and Mia hadn't wanted to stress her more. So Mia had simply assumed—*wrongly*—that the 'S' in all those emails stood for Santo. It didn't. It was Sante with an 'e.' She knew *exactly* who he was and she was no longer warring between melting and freezing; she was numb.

He stood more rigid than ever, glaring at her with that outrageously square jaw while she chewed. It took a while before she could swallow because it had been a good third of the pastry that she'd shoved in there. The tragedy was she'd couldn't even taste it anymore. It could've been cardboard for all the pleasure it brought. Of course she shouldn't have done it, but she'd needed to buy time to work out how on earth she was going to deal with the devil before her.

Sante Trovato couldn't decide if he was hallucinating or this was real because apparently Venus herself had materialised in his bathroom. *Bountiful* was a word. *Mag-*

nificent another. Half-dressed and luscious and looking *him* up and down with hungry, wide blue eyes as if he...

His mouth dried. He'd visually drowned in acres of creamy skin and ample curves, in the tempting richness of the long chocolate-brown hair cascading over her shoulder. As for her consumption of that custard pastry—she'd inhaled the remainder like some sex goddess. She was *all* goddess and—

He could not be thinking these thoughts.

Gritting his teeth, he slammed the brakes on his brain, but still couldn't help absorbing her beauty. With high heels she would look him almost straight in the eye, and he was tall. She was all curves and straights and *fascinating.* Sante could only stare.

Was he in a dream he couldn't wake from? He'd returned to Rome late last night, come straight to the office, gotten stuck in to a problem and worked through the night. He thought he'd woken fifteen minutes ago with a minor headache and a dry throat, figured a quick shower would help, but here he was still asleep and—

'Tell me who you are,' he muttered in a strangled voice.

The only way to be sure she was real was to reach out and touch her. His muscles tensed in anticipation of pleasure. He gritted his teeth harder as she licked another scrap of pastry from her lower lip.

'Would you mind turning away?' she said.

Her tone was absolutely frigid.

Sante instinctively rebelled. He'd seen her looking at him with heat and hunger so what had caused the sea-change in her emotion? For a split second he stared longer, then reality jolted and he stalked out of the bathroom.

He stood in the centre of his office and buttoned his shirt to the collar.

What had happened? What had she suddenly thought that made her turn to ice? He stiffened as the old defensiveness swept over him. He hadn't been verbally disciplined in a decade but she'd spoken with the same cold tone of the English school principal of the boarding school he'd been sent to. He remembered the day his hopes for a life-changing education had been destroyed. Sante had rejected the sought-after university scholarship before the offer could be rescinded. He'd been blamed for an accident. His innocence was irrelevant. Sante had *always* been blamed. Guys who came from backgrounds like his always were, no matter the truth. Which was why he'd built his own company. Why he still operated alone as much as possible. He had a few property and investment assistants for his portfolio and recently gathered a small group of techs to work through the ideas that wouldn't let his brain rest. But none spoke to him the way this woman just had. No one did. Not *now*. Not since he'd taken complete control of his life and expunged his past. So who was she and why was she taking off her blouse in his private restroom? His brain didn't actually care. His brain just wanted to go back in there and drink in her luscious curves. He'd been caught off guard and he was stupid tired…

No excuses. He was at *work*. He would focus on her prim disapproval, not her succulent body. Not that smear of cream on her shirt nor the appetite with which she'd demolished the pastry. He would not think about the slide of her tongue across her full lips and not her radiant, smooth skin that his fingertips itched to touch. He wouldn't focus on any of that. He wouldn't allow such a distraction to destroy his equilibrium or his reputation. He planted himself in front of his desk, legs apart, arms folded, and glared at the door, waiting for her to emerge.

'Who are you and what are you doing here?' he demanded the second she walked out.

Her new shirt was buttoned to the base of her creamy neck but the copious material didn't hide the curvaceous body beneath. He made himself focus on her face, blinking as a vague thought stirred in the back of his still-distracted brain. Yes, her mood had gone from hunger to hatred but there was something about the set of her eyes that made him pause. Not just their stunning clarity but—

'Adele hired me to run the office while she attends to a personal matter,' she said in that annoyingly precise and prim way. 'She didn't want to disturb you. Apparently, you don't like that.'

'What?' He frowned. There'd been fewer emails from his office manager than usual but Adele knew his preferred method and frequency of communication. 'I've been at a conference—'

'That ended five days ago. Weekdays that is,' the curvy brunette interrupted icily. 'There's been a weekend in the middle as well.'

He stiffened. Who was this woman to judge his routine? Sante loathed judgement of all forms. He often was away for days at a stretch, and he relied on Adele to keep things ticking along as she had for nearly the past *nine years*. This was normal for them and why he'd given her full oversight over the office. But if there was a problem, Adele would've definitely made contact. Admittedly, he'd gone deep into a contemplative hole this past week but the fact that his assistant hadn't bothered him surely meant that whatever the problem was, it couldn't be that bad. 'How long does she need off?'

'Adele hired me to act as office manager for the next three months.'

He reeled. *That* wasn't happening. He couldn't have this walking distraction near him for that long. 'And I'm supposed to just take your word for that?'

'If you'd bothered to come into the office, or even, I don't know, picked up your phone to personally talk to any one of your staff, then you'd already know.'

Her chastening tone irritated him. He *had* missed a call from Adele a few days ago and he'd not had a chance to return it. He'd emailed through various instructions as normal, though. And gotten a reply. But now he wondered who the reply had been from. He swallowed uncomfortably. Why hadn't Adele emailed about this? Or tried calling again? The older woman had been his first hire and still was his most reliable, loyal employee, so much so he'd given her leeway in the office set-up. She'd directly hired half those young techs and her instincts were usually good. The last thing he wanted was to lose her. She sorted any office issues before they were even brought to his attention. But maybe that was what she'd tried to do here.

'Adele was almost as worried about inconveniencing you as she was worried about Bruno,' the brunette beauty added in his silence.

Any last lingering haze of sexual arousal still enveloping Sante evaporated in a blink. 'What's wrong with Bruno?' he snapped.

'He's had a stroke.'

'*What?*' Sante leaned back on the edge of his desk, his

legs emptying of strength in the shock. Why hadn't Adele been in touch when it had been this serious? 'When?'

'Adele can't have any more stress or *she'll* become unwell,' she added. 'If you knew her, you'd know that.'

Of *course* he knew that! 'She should have come to me. I would have given her—'

'And if you *really* knew her, you'd know she wouldn't ever ask for or accept your charity.'

But he did know that, too, because he *did* know his very efficient executive. Okay, perhaps not all that well personally because that was how both he and Adele preferred it. She was efficient, discreet, reliable. She worked exact hours—she never would have turned up as early as this—yet she got absolutely everything done. Always. Adele was the perfect employee. Or she had been until hiring *this* woman as her temporary replacement in the office. He was not the bad guy here.

'Or is leaving people to suffer alone your forte?'

Sante went very still as his pulse suddenly roared in his ears. The creamy-skinned brunette was unnaturally still, too. He mentally repeated her soft accusation several times until it sank in. Then he stepped forward and grabbed her arm because he still needed to be sure. '*What* did you just say?'

Mia shouldn't have said it but her tongue had run away before her brain could catch it. She *hated* this man. With her heart and soul she hated him. Sante Trovato had ruined *years* of her brother's life. Because of him her brother Dario had *suffered* so much. He'd endured physical pain, emotional betrayal and he'd lost so much time. And now Sante was her temporary boss and looking every inch the ruthless billionaire that he was. His presence was shocking enough, but that she'd felt an appallingly intense moment of sexual attraction to *him* was horrifying.

'Who are you?' His voice was still barely above a whisper, yet every menacing word reverberated to her bones.

Except it wasn't only her bones that responded. She was so weakened by him she didn't even try to jerk her upper arm free of his grip—and he wasn't even holding her that tightly. His strength was leashed and he still held back from giving her the oddly disconcerting feeling of being too close yet distanced. The insane thing was for a split second she wanted him *closer*. He was unbelievably handsome—no wonder it had taken her a moment to recognise him. Sante had gone from a lanky teen with close-cropped hair to a tall, muscular man whose tousled hair had an untameable life to it.

Mia cleared her throat, trying to rationalise that her attraction was merely from the surprise—she'd not expected to see a bare-chested man in the office, definitely not such a built one, and as she'd not seen let alone touched a guy in a long, long while, that moment had simply been a basic physiological response to masculine beauty. Animal instinct. She was over it already. Except she needed him to release her and step back. He didn't. He just stepped closer still.

'*Who* are you?' He ground the question, a muscle jumping in his jaw.

She was filled with remorse for not asking Adele all those finer details. For being arrogant enough to assume she could handle a job she was barely qualified for. But *this* man was even more arrogant. He thought he could do whatever he wanted and get away with it. He was a cold-blooded, avaricious ass who cared only about himself and his money. Most of all, he was a *coward*.

And she would not cower before him. She stiffened, trying to tug her arm free. 'Ms Simonini. I'm your new office manager.'

His eyes narrowed and he still didn't release her. She knew he wouldn't recognise that surname—it was her maternal grandfather's; she'd rejected her family name the moment she'd turned eighteen.

'Okay, Ms Simonini, what did you mean about me leaving people alone to suffer?'

'What do you think I meant?' She swallowed.

He put profit and prospects before people. Before loyalty. He was a *user* and he would cheat to win.

'You're English.' He dropped his hold on her so suddenly she had to take a step back to keep her balance.

She immediately rallied and stepped forward again. 'Actually, I'm half Italian.'

He stared into her face. His brain ticking over. It took him so long to place her it was almost an insult.

'Mia,' he muttered. His head lifted and he snapped. 'You're not Simonini, you're...*Lorenti*. You're Dario Lorenti's sister.' He inhaled sharply. 'You can pack your things and leave immediately.'

'Why?' She held fast. 'Does my presence cause you guilt? Shame, perhaps? I should hope so.'

Her brother would completely freak out if he knew who she was standing in front of now. Which meant he wasn't about to find out. This was only a three-month contract and she was never letting Sante Trovato intimidate her out of here just because her presence prickled his conscience. So it damned well should.

He folded his arms across his chest and glared at her. 'Whatever offer Adele made you, its terminated.'

Yeah, no. Mia didn't let anyone tell her what she could or couldn't do. Not anymore. And she was not going to make this easy for him by walking out of here and not looking back. She was not doing that to Adele. She was not doing that to her brother.

'*I'm* not going anywhere.' She stepped close, suddenly determined to thwart the jerk.

While she and Dario weren't as close as she'd like, the opportunity to be the thorn in the side of his sworn enemy was too good to pass up. She'd been too young to defend Dario properly back then. Or to be an ally against their horror of a father. But she was different now and this was one fight she wasn't backing down from.

'I signed a fixed contract with Adele,' she said. '*You* can't simply terminate it.'

That muscle ticked in his jaw again. 'I think you'll find I'm—'

'Obliged to observe employment laws just like everybody else.'

'No.' He inhaled sharply. 'You're done. Don't worry, I'll ensure you're paid until the end of the week.'

Of course he thought he could just get his way. He *always* got his own way. He was the most selfish man in existence. He even trounced her father in that arena, which was really an achievement.

'You're dismissing me on what grounds?' she asked.

There were a few tense moments as he glared at her.

'Gross misconduct,' he eventually bit.

'What?'

'Stripping in the office. This is no place for sexual impropriety.'

Oh, he had to be kidding! Mia lifted her chin. She'd been slut shamed by her father simply for developing breasts and she wasn't having it here. 'Says the man who was *equally* undressed.'

'Because it was *my* office bathroom. You walked un-announced in there and started stripping.'

'Only in your wildest dreams would I have done that had I known you were there.'

For a split second an unreadable emotion flickered in his eyes. It almost looked like amusement. 'Okay, then you're suspended on suspicion of corporate espionage.'

'Excuse me?' Mia gaped at him.

'You're in here spying for your brother.'

Well, that was the most outrageous and infuriating thing she'd ever heard because Sante Trovato was the true *thief* around here. 'My brother doesn't need to steal anything from you.'

'Because he has all that inherited wealth?' Sante said acidly. 'That wouldn't stop him trying. People like your brother can never have enough.'

She was speechless. Sante Trovato was the greedy one. He was the morally dubious. *Never* her brother.

'There's no other reason for you to be in my private domain,' he added.

'I had no idea it was your private domain. If I'd *known* I wouldn't be within fifty feet of anything, anyone or any *place* to do with you,' she said scornfully.

'So much ferocity merely confirms my theory that you're in here spying.'

'I came in here to change my shirt.' She ground her teeth.

'That's your convenient excuse in case you were caught. The likelihood of which would be low given how early you're at work. Quite the enthusiastic assistant, aren't you? So *eager* to please. It's a very good facade for falsehood.'

'The likelihood of my being caught is only low because neither you nor your supposedly genius workers like to actually show up to work.'

'So you admit you're in here snooping.'

'Of course I *wasn't*. I just wanted to change my shirt—'

'Because you're a messy eater?'

'Sometimes, yes. Absolutely.' And she wasn't ashamed nor afraid to admit it.

He blinked. 'There's another bathroom for the workers. This one is mine.'

'As I'd thought the boss was permanently AWOL, I figured it was okay to change in here. The other bathroom is ages away from my desk and I didn't want to traipse all the way through the office dropping more cream.'

'Why don't you use your true surname? What are you trying to hide?' he asked.

'Unlike you I have nothing to hide.'

He looked furious all over again.

Good. Mia used a different name because she didn't want to be associated with her father—not that he'd ever bothered to bestow *his* name on them legally. But she didn't want to ride on her *brother's* success, either. She preferred to avoid the assumptions when people found out her connections. She liked her independence. But now she smiled. 'Maybe I'm married.'

Fire flashed in his eyes and he quickly glanced at her unadorned hands. 'Constantly lying to my face really isn't going to help your employment case.'

'Don't you ever read your emails?' she asked coolly, determined to get this conversation back on track.

She was even more determined not to leave. She would happily cause his conscience problems for a few weeks with her presence. She was a connection to his past and he immediately wanted to get rid of her. Too bad for him.

His lips thinned. 'How bad is Bruno?' There was a beat. 'Adele should know I would h—' He broke off and cleared his throat.

At the starkness flashing in his eyes, Mia could *almost* believe he was genuinely concerned. But she already knew the man had neither conscience nor heart.

'Why didn't she get in touch with me?' he asked quietly after a moment. 'She only called once.'

'If you hadn't disappeared off the planet, maybe she would have tried again. But you'd vanished and apparently when that happens, you can't be disturbed—no matter the circumstances. It's written all in caps and underscored three times in the tip sheet she left for me after our handover here.'

He blinked. 'You had a handover here?'

'Of course I did. Adele loves this job and she did the best she could in the time she had because she was afraid of disappointing her insanely demanding boss.'

She completely failed to understand why Adele would want to work for him—but clearly, Adele didn't know what Mia knew. The truth.

'How long have you been working here?' he asked.

'Almost two weeks.'

He looked both horrified and apoplectic. 'You've had access to this office for two weeks?'

'Plus Adele's email. Yes.'

'That's a gross breach of confidentiality.'

'Oh? Why don't you want your new office manager to access company data? What have you got to hide?'

She'd seen his emails. They were unbelievably devoid of any human element. It was lists of tasks. No praise. No personal chat. Nothing remotely nice or supportive or checking in that Adele and the rest of the staff were okay.

'Oh, I know.' She smiled viciously. 'You don't want the world to know what a traitorous jerk you really are. Is that why you keep your name so discreetly hidden from all company documents?'

He simply stared at her. Not rising to her provocation. That Adele had referred to him as Saint was too ironic.

'You don't want anyone to find out your shameful secret,' she said, her fury rising.

'What secret do you think that is?'

Was he serious? Did he really want her to spell it out? She'd *been* there. She'd witnessed it all. But fine. She'd play his game.

'That you're a fraud.' She locked her knees to stop them trembling. 'You're a liar. You're a cheat. And you're a callous coward.'

He didn't move. He just whispered. 'And you know this because…'

'You caused the accident that almost killed my brother. You ran away, leaving him trapped, injured, alone. And then you stole his ideas to make your first billion using my father's blood money as your seed capital. You like a payout, Sante. And all the while he was suffering. Dario suffered for *years*.'

Sante reared back as if she'd whipped him.

Good.

Mia breathed hard. Her brother Dario *still* suffered. What had happened back then had changed him. It had changed everything. And it was entirely Sante Trovato's fault.

Her fury unleashed, Mia jabbed her hand on his chest to emphasise her words. 'You're a shark who'll destroy anyone who gets in your way. But not this time. You're *not* getting rid of me.'

CHAPTER TWO

SANTE TROVATO TENSED as rage ricocheted through him. Again. If he didn't hold himself on lock he'd forcibly manhandle her out of the building or, worse, silence her in another diabolically inappropriate way involving their mouths. He was giving in to *neither* of those impulses.

Stolen her brother's idea? Taken blood money from her father?

She was utterly deluded. But her accusations stirred memories he'd ruthlessly suppressed for years, and his head spun as he struggled to catch up on a catastrophe he'd not seen coming.

'Is that what you think happened?' he muttered tightly.

'It's what I know happened. I was there.'

Hatred radiated from her. Dario Lorenti's little sister was hissing like an aggravated kitten, fury pushing her not only to provoke him, but punish him as well. To make him *pay*.

Just over ten years ago, he'd been at boarding school in the UK with Dario. They'd been friends then. As close as Sante had been to anyone. They'd busted out of school one weekend— gone to a music festival. But Sante had gotten lost on a back country road in Wales. It was black as pitch and he'd slowed—but not enough. He'd lost almost everything in that instant. But what Mia thought had happened was a shockingly far-fetched twisted version of the truth.

He hadn't taken her damned father's money, but he *had* been the driver in the crash that had almost killed her brother and smashed his leg. And no, it didn't matter that Sante had modelled the physics of the crash on a computer over and over again and knew, fully *knew*, that there was no way he could have avoided it, he still felt guilty about it. He would always feel guilty about it. Just as he would always feel guilty about not protecting his foster brother years earlier. Those facts proved he wasn't meant to be around people much, but he was too on edge, too defensive, to explain any of that to *her*.

'If I'm such a monster, why do you want to work for me?' He glared at her, ignoring the intense pull he felt towards her on a molecular level. He was not touching her again. Never *ever*.

'Let me repeat it for you one more time. Slowly.' She glared back, adding an even more patronising inflection to her irritatingly precise intonation. Her Italian was laced by that posh English accent, instantly giving away her status. 'I'm not working for *you*, I'm working for Adele. *She's* the reason I'm not leaving.'

As if she were some holier-than-thou saviour stepping in to protect his best, most highly paid, most trusted until *now*, employee from his appalling treatment?

'*I* won't let *her* down,' she added, tightening the screws.

Mia couldn't claim the moral high ground. She was a *Lorenti*, and the greed and ruthlessness she'd just assigned to him was nothing on that of her own family. A fact which made Sante certain that playing protector to

Adele *wasn't* her only motive now. Bitten as he was by the urge to toss her onto the street, he would find out her intentions first, then neutralise her.

He scooped up his phone. 'Then let's see what she says.'

He'd initially thought that as Adele hadn't pushed to get hold of him, it meant that whatever had happened wasn't that bad. Now he knew the truth was the total opposite. Bruno had to be desperately unwell because while Sante had given her a lot of power, Adele would never normally hire someone to step into the office without at least consulting him.

He stared at Mia as he waited for Adele to answer, trying not to feel a hit that Adele hadn't confided in him. But he didn't have *personal* relationships with employees. Not with anyone, in fact. He'd dated on and off over the years before remembering that he hated the prying into his past that inevitably eventually occurred. So now he was a misanthropic loner who had the occasional one-night stand and that was the way he liked it. He had plenty of projects and properties to occupy him. But Adele had been his only employee for the first few years, and she'd stuck with him all this time and she hadn't told him she was in trouble.

Of course she'd stuck with him only because he paid well. But he paid her well because she was intelligent and reliable. Until now, when she'd hired the sister of his enemy. Not that Mia was a threat to him in any kind of murderous way, but her presence forced Sante to revisit a deep injustice he couldn't stand to consider let alone resolve. Adele wouldn't have known anything about that when she'd contracted Mia. Sante—and Mia's father—had worked in their own very different ways to ensure that.

Adele finally answered his call and the second she did he heard the strain in her voice. He immediately regretted doing this in front of Mia. He'd wanted to see her squirm; instead, he was the one feeling wretchedly uncomfortable. He met Mia's cool blue gaze as he offered what he could for Adele—money, more resources—and clenched his teeth when Adele distractedly assured him everything was okay and that she just needed time and that she was so sorry for letting him down but that she knew Mia would be doing a wonderful job for him. Hearing her anxiety, Sante could only bite harder before confirming that indeed Mia was, and that he would be in touch again soon.

Mia's chin lifted in triumph. But Sante couldn't contradict Adele or subject her to a barrage of questions when she was so obviously masking her distress. He ended the call, even more frustrated. Adele wouldn't accept direct help. He'd have to figure a more creative way to ensure she had all the support she needed. He would also have to discover all he needed to know about Mia directly from her. Given her attitude, he was going to have to watch her every move.

'Did you find out what you needed to know?' Sparks flickered in Mia's eyes, enhancing their blue.

Sante surveyed her defiant stance with bitter, fatalistic amusement. 'Not everything. I need your résumé.'

'I'm already hired.' She folded her arms across her chest.

Sante wished she hadn't. It had been a defensive gesture but all it did was enhance her glorious shape.

Focus. He cleared his throat and distracted himself

by picking up a pen. 'For now, but I'd like to understand exactly what Adele saw that she thought you'd be such a perfect fit.'

She took another step into his office—filling up all his vision and causing maximum discomfort.

'Adele has worked for you for almost a decade and never let you down.'

'She didn't know who you *really* are,' he muttered acidly. 'You deceived her.'

'You still think that was some elaborate plot?'

'I don't believe she told you how long she's been with me but didn't tell you my name.' He stepped forward to expend just a smidge of the extra energy racing round his body.

'She only ever refers to you as *Saint*. It's like a bad joke.'

Sante glared at her. Adele did call him that and it *was* a joke between them. About the only one they had.

While it ought to be unbelievable that Mia hadn't known who she'd be working for when talking with Adele, it was *possible*. Sante fiercely guarded his privacy—everything personal about him was locked down both online and off—but not for the insulting fabricated reasons she'd inventoried earlier.

'I still want a copy of your résumé,' he said coldly.

Mia Lorenti came from a family of users who thought money could buy them anything they wanted. Why did she even need to work? Hadn't her jerk father left her a few million when he'd died a few years back—making Dario some pretentious duke or lord or the like? It galled Sante that he even knew this much. Maybe Mia had partied her way through her inheritance already. Well, she wouldn't be in his offices by the end of the day. *He* would pay *her* off if he had to—whether he'd have to buy out her entire contract or offer more, he didn't care. The Lorenti family was all about money, so it was only a matter of meeting her greed. Then she would be gone and he would forget that searing moment of sensual attraction.

'I'll email it as soon as I have a minute.'

'You have a minute now.'

She pinned him with those ice-blue eyes and lowered her voice. 'Try to make life difficult for me and I'll sue you for constructive dismissal.'

He almost smiled. 'I see you have your father's negotiation skills.'

'I'm *nothing* like my father.' Stiff with outrage, she stalked out.

Sante stared after her. Well, *that* got a reaction. Scoring a hit felt good because her fictional list of *his* supposed failings earlier had bruised. Why should he care what she chose to believe? He rubbed his temples and turned back to his desk.

In the bathroom before, he'd seen fury bloom in her eyes as it had slowly dawned on her *who* he was. She'd eventually *recognised* him. Because they'd met before. He forced himself not to consider the curves he'd glimpsed, but to think back to the eighteen months he'd spent in the UK that had changed his life.

He'd spent one summer at Westwick, her father's stately pile in Wiltshire. At the time Sante would have said it was the best summer of his life—certainly, it had been his *only* holiday. The only time he'd had away from the boarding school aside from sports tournaments. A few months before the accident in their final school year, it had been a summer of freedom. He and Dario had spent the afternoons training for sport, learning to code on Dario's computers half the night and spitballing app ideas—the more ludicrous the better. He'd naively believed he might finally have a future he could look forward to. Dario had been his best friend—hell, he'd have considered him the brother he'd never had apart from—*no*. He slammed the door on that earlier, even more devastating, memory. He could *never* go there.

Dario's father had come home twice during that summer and his presence had instantly changed the atmosphere of the place. But there'd been another occupant in the house aside from the stand-offish, clearly disapproving, staff. Mia Lorenti. At least five years younger than Dario, she'd been a rambunctious kid with long, messy hair, loud laughter and who sang as she skipped down the long corridors of the manor. He'd not interacted much with her, he'd been busy plotting with Dario, but he finally let himself remember the last time he'd been face-to-face with her. She'd been in the reception area of the hospital when Sante had finally made it there a full twelve hours after the crash. She'd been tired, tear-stained, so young and he'd asked her how Dario was. She'd not known.

But she'd clearly believed whatever she'd been told about him since.

Stolen idea... Blood money...

He swallowed the bitter betrayal at the scope of the lies her father had spun. Sante had no real *need* to defend himself, yet he felt oddly compelled to. It would be a futile undertaking. It wasn't as if he could just tell her and expect that she would believe him. People *always* believed the worst. And he refused to have her opinion matter.

She wasn't a kid now. Now she was tall, curvaceous, utterly beautiful and utterly unable to be ignored in any way.

He wasn't actually attracted to her. He'd just experienced a basic bodily reaction to copping an eyeful of breasts spilling over lace bra cups—unexpected, and his reaction had been visceral. Automatic. Frankly, animal. Because he'd had barely any sleep and his brain had gone primeval on him because of it.

Frustratedly, he refreshed his email. No CV. So much for the efficiency everyone was raving about. Still, the longer she took to fulfil his request, the better, right? If she failed in her duties he could get rid of her even more quickly.

In that instant his email pinged a notification. Mia's CV. He read the document five times and was no less apoplectic by the end of the ninety seconds that it took. He snatched up the phone again.

'Get back in here,' he ordered gruffly.

She appeared in the doorway in moments. Chin high, the epitome of spiky defiance.

'Do you order all your employees about with such devastating charm?' she asked. 'No wonder none of them like to make an appearance in the office.'

Sante chose to use few words at the best of times but to be actually rendered speechless was new, even for him. And he pushed against it.

'Close the door.' He cleared the gruffness from his throat.

Her eyebrows lifted.

'Unless you want everyone to overhear how spectacularly unqualified you are to work for me,' he elaborated.

'We both know I'm far *too* qualified.' She closed the door and leaned against it. 'Aside from the lawyer to keep you out of jail, your accountant to track your ill-gotten billions and an older woman you take advantage of because she's desperate to support her unwell husband, you only employ university dropouts and ex-hackers—none of whom are actually present right now.'

Sante gaped, then clamped his mouth shut. It seemed Mia had no problem in using many words—albeit unwisely. She was being deliberately and outrageously provocative and to his utter bemusement he suddenly felt the urge to laugh. *Not* an appropriate reaction, and he dragged up an element of severity. 'You were a *nanny*.'

Amongst an assortment of other temporary and vastly different jobs in a variety of places. But Mia was basically British aristocracy, so why had she spent the past five years working an assortment of weird and frankly low-paying jobs using an alternate surname?

'Yes.' Fire flickered in her eyes and she lifted her chin proudly. 'I was a very good one. I have the employer recommendations to prove it. Feel free to phone and check them.'

Mia crossed her fingers behind her back. Sante Trovato was calling her bluff but she was bluffing right back. Still smarting from the humiliation of standing in front of him while he'd spoken with Adele, she wasn't letting any weakness show.

Adele had made her 'saint' of a boss sound ancient and somewhat infirm. She'd said he spent a lot of time working from his private estate and that he needed gentle handling. It was complete rot. Sante Trovato was an absolute villain. He'd left her brother trapped in a smashed-up car on a country road in the middle of the night. He'd been Dario's friend, then taken so much from him.

She *did* have exemplary references from every job other than the first. She'd fudged the embarrassing end to that one but she'd learned her lesson. Never again would she make the mortifying mistake of having an affair at work.

Ordinarily, she would be the first to admit she wasn't perfect. As a child she'd been full of mischief, but after her mother's death she'd moved to her father's home in England and become 'always makes mistakes Mia.' As the old jerk had repeatedly berated, she was too boister-ous, too capricious, too loud, too much. But while she was well used to never pleasing authority figures, *Sante* was no saint and his searingly obvious judgement stirred her full rebellion.

Mia had long ago accepted there was no real way to ease the pain Dario had suffered, but maybe she could make Sante pay just a little.

He rose and walked around his desk, slowly advancing upon her with a thoughtful expression in his eyes. 'My employees are not toddlers.'

'No, but they have some traits in common with the little darlings,' she said. 'They like to nap. Take time out to play. Have the occasional tantrum.'

His lips twisted. 'Are you stereotyping my coders?'

She shrugged. 'I've managed recalcitrant children. I've managed egotistical genius chefs in a five-star restaurant and exhausted crew on a ship coping with overly demand-ing wealthy clients in the middle of a ten-week luxury cruise. I can handle your teenagers.'

His jaw flicked. Was he about to *smile*?

The man had a shocking amount of magnetism despite his grumpy demeanour. Good-looking even when frowning, his rare flash of a smile was electrifying. Looks like his were actually a weapon.

She stiffened even more. 'I can pull people together.'

'You think I want you to pull them together?'

'Adele said that you wanted to get your workers into the office for the same two days in a week, isn't that correct?' she asked. 'I'll create an environment in which they can thrive.'

Mia was neither daunted nor fazed by that challenge. She knew how to treat spoiled children. But Sante Trovato was more than spoiled. He was selfish and he had no empathy.

He blinked. 'That was something she and I discussed.'

'Well, it might be helpful if the CEO were to lead by example.'

'You're saying you want *me* in the office?'

'I've been here ten days and this is the first one you've bothered to show up.'

He glared at her. 'I have no immediate travel plans. You have ideas for bringing them back in?'

'I have a plan,' she fudged.

'Talk me through it.'

'I prefer to show, not tell.' She was fully employing delaying tactics.

'Actions over words?' He cocked his head. 'Do you really think I'm going to let *you* do whatever you want with my workers?'

Why did that sound inappropriate? She arched her eyebrows at him. 'Maybe you should. Give me rope to hang myself, right? Then you can fire me legitimately without having to resort to threatening behaviour.'

'How did you meet Adele?'

'I was the activities coordinator on a cruise she and Bruno were on a couple of years ago.'

'A cruise?'

She bristled at his obvious distaste. No doubt Sante would hire a luxury yacht and ensure he never had to see any staff, the supercilious jerk.

'A big one with a lot of customers and a lot of activities to coordinate. I'm extremely good with spreadsheets and rosters.'

'It was a cruise to Norway.'

'Yes.' She was taken aback. She'd not had the impression he would know anything about it. 'We got on very well. I always thought it a shame that she had to work most of the time she was on board.'

Sante's lips twisted into a small cynical smile. 'I paid for that cruise outside of her usual remuneration. Adele only accepted on the proviso she would work while she was away. Adele loves her job. She's been with me for years.'

'I know. It's a true mystery as to why.'

His lips twisted. 'Perhaps I'm a good boss.'

'Well, you *are* out of the office more often than not...' Mia mused. 'I suppose that would be a bonus.'

'Just so you know, I barely bothered her during that cruise. I didn't actually ask her for anything while she was away so any work she did, she did out of her own sense of responsibility. In fact, in the end I had to get one of my techs to lock her out of the company intranet for a couple of days just to be sure she would actually have a break, and even then she was on the phone to me complaining about it. That cruise was the only way Bruno was ever going to see the Northern Lights,' he muttered. 'I offered her the jet but as you already know, not only is Adele extremely good at her job, she's irritatingly proud. She wouldn't just take a gift. She wanted to earn it and pay for it all herself but his medical costs were draining her savings, so that was the compromise we agreed on. She's my best employee and I would—'

He broke off and growled.

Mia stared as he ran his hand through his hair and turned away from her. He looked and sounded sincere and for a moment she almost believed him. Adele was important to him. Yet, he'd gone off for days with no word and Adele hadn't wanted to bother him?

He turned that hard, bottomless gaze back on her. 'So you befriended Adele on board?'

Straight back to sceptical and suspicious.

'Actually, I made friends with Bruno first. He's an absolute gentleman and in her view that put her in my debt.'

He nodded.

'So we both want her to focus on him now and not worry about what's happening in here,' Mia said.

He studied her. 'Are you able to set aside your loathing and work for me?'

'I'm able to do my best for Adele. Also your workers. They deserve that.'

His eyebrows lifted. 'You feel sorry for them?'

'You only want your disparate group of brilliant coders and creatives to work together more so they'll spit out more ideas for you to add to your billions. Like some kind of genius factory.'

'Because you think I'm incapable of having my own ideas?'

'You stole them in the past. I guess at least here you're paying them.'

His eyes kindled. 'Why do you need to work at all?' he asked softly. 'Didn't your father leave you millions?'

She'd never taken anything from her father. Not even in his death. And she flared against the suggestion that she ever would. '*You* took more money from that man than I ever did.'

'Did I?'

'Yes,' she hissed. 'He paid you off after you crashed the car and ran away leaving Dario for dead.'

The difference between her and Sante was that he would take money. It was all that mattered to him. He would jettison any person to get it and keep it. But Mia needed autonomy and independence and to earn her own. She'd rather starve in the streets than take anything from her father. A few times she almost had.

Sante didn't seem to move. 'Is that what he told you happened?'

She didn't need to be told. 'That *is* what happened. I was there.'

'You *saw* me take your father's money?' he asked dryly.

She stiffened. No, she hadn't actually *seen* the actual transaction. But that didn't mean it hadn't happened. 'You're telling me it didn't?'

'Why would I bother? It's not like you'd believe me.'

Right. Because Mia hadn't just heard things. She'd *seen* things. She'd been there back then and he couldn't deny they'd happened just by turning his soulful brown eyes on her.

'You ran away from the accident,' she said. 'You ran,' she added. 'I *saw* you when they finally caught you and brought you to the hospital—'

'I ran to get *help*,' he interrupted bluntly. 'I just ran in the wrong damned direction.'

Mia froze at the underlying fury in Sante's goaded tone. Dario hadn't remembered anything about the accident. Her father had relayed to her brother what the doctor had said. What the police had said. What their school principal had said. Her father had been the filter for *everything* both Dario and she had known about the accident and the aftermath. Except for what Mia had actually seen, and she *had* seen Sante that terrible morning. He'd been scared. He'd sounded guilty. He'd kept saying he was *sorry*.

She dragged in a breath. 'You were pale—'

'I was *fine*.'

She might've been young but even she'd known Sante was anything but fine. He'd come to stay at Westwick for the summer only a few months earlier. He'd taken up all Dario's time and Mia had been left on her own. She'd hated Sante for that. But honestly, she'd also been fascinated by her brother's dark-eyed, quiet friend. At the hospital she'd initially been pleased to see him. She'd been alone in the reception area for hours. Lonely. Hungry. Not understanding how unwell Dario really was but afraid he'd disappear from her life like their mother had. That everything would change again and she would be alone for good. Because her father was no real father.

When Sante had been brought in she'd been too young

to ask the right questions, to even understand what was going on. But she'd noticed his bloodied socks. The dried sweat and dirt, his pale face and the panic in his eyes.

'He said you caused the accident,' Mia muttered.

'Dario—?'

'Dario couldn't remember anything about that night. My father said that's what the police said.'

His gaze didn't waver from hers. 'Then why wasn't I charged over it?'

'Because Dad wanted to protect Dario from the stress of a trial. He needed time and space to recover.' Including from her. 'My father told the police not to prosecute you.'

'And you think he was powerful enough to influence justice like that?'

Yes. But her breathing grew uneven. Her father was wealthy—might have thought he could control everything— but perhaps he *didn't* have that power? The police would have charged. In fact, knowing her father, he would have *insisted* on it. Which meant he'd have been even more angry if there were no case to answer.

'He said you were expelled from school. He said you took the money. That you agreed to stay away from Dario.'

'*I* left the school before they could expel me. I didn't take a cent from your father. I would never let someone else dictate who I could be friends with.'

She couldn't believe him yet his assertiveness seeded the smallest of doubts.

'Did Dario say I'd stolen his idea?' Sante asked tightly.

'You talked about coding and ideas all the time that summer.'

'Not my app. He lied if he said we discussed that.'

Mia stared at him. Dario had been in recovery a long

time. She'd been kept away from him. Ultimately, he'd become distanced from *everyone*.

'He doesn't talk about you,' Mia admitted.

'So you came to that wildly inaccurate conclusion all by yourself,' Sante said acidly.

'My brother and I are separate people,' she said stiffly.

'So he really doesn't know who you're working for?'

'*I* didn't know who I was working for until just over an hour ago,' she reiterated with annoyance. 'Dario has no idea where I am. We haven't spoken in a few months.'

'Why not?'

She gritted her teeth because she'd not wanted to open up as much as she had to him. 'Adele and I have independence in common.'

'You mean you won't do whatever it is he wants you to.'

Given his audible judgement of Dario, she didn't want to admit that Sante was right. But Dario wasn't anything like her father. He wanted what was *best* for her.

Sante watched her dispassionately. 'Are you going to tell him you're working for me?'

'He doesn't need to know. He's not my keeper.' She needed to move forward, to get enough space to think all this through properly. 'Dario is irrelevant now. As is my father. There's no need for us to discuss anything personal ever again.'

He looked sceptical. 'Can you work for me if you believe I would take a pay-off?'

'My personal opinion of you won't impact on my ability to do my job,' she said. 'I can be professional.'

Slowly, he stepped towards her.

'But you don't want me here,' she muttered, annoyance

growing as he towered over her. 'Because you don't want anyone to know the truth about your past.'

'Is this the part where you demand payment for your silence?'

She stayed still, refusing to be intimidated into backing away from him. 'That's your playbook, not mine.'

'So you're not here to do anything other than—'

'Help Adele. I made a commitment to her and I'm going to see it through. I'm going to do a good job.'

He stopped an inch away from being too close. 'I'll give you one week to prove it.'

'You'll give me my entire contracted time and I'm not the one with innocence to prove.'

'But, Mia.' He shot her a bitter smile. 'Isn't it *guilt* that normally requires proving?'

CHAPTER THREE

MIA ROLLED HER eyes and stalked to her desk. The nerve of the guy; he was totally guilty and they both knew it. Almost the second she'd sat down, her phone rang. It was a stressed Adele, checking Sante was okay and telling Mia not to let him try to do anything for her and Bruno. Mia couldn't understand how Adele could work for someone as soulless as Sante let alone be so desperate not to cause *him* any additional trouble. She just managed to stop herself calling out the older woman for *coddling* the jerk and managed to reassure her instead. She would take care of it. But the way they treated him was ridiculous. Mia wasn't about to do the same. She would work hard, but she wouldn't succumb to whatever spell he'd put on all his other workers. It seemed the coders were clearly affected. Mattia was the only one who'd arrived this morning, but the second he'd seen Sante was present he'd sent out an alert. Four more had arrived in the past hour. They didn't look scared. They were *excited*. It seemed *everyone* in the office was amped that Sante had finally shown up. But the man stayed in his office, his door imperiously shut firm. However, as the office was all wooden floors and exposed brick and glass, a procession of staff wandered past, peeking to catch a glimpse of the rare and magical creature. Sante Trovato was apparently a unicorn. He'd somehow manipulated them into thinking he was something wonderful. No doubt his looks helped. The lean youth who'd taken her brother away had matured into an impossibly handsome man with unruly hair and bottomless brown eyes. The sharp cheekbones, sculpted jaw and loose-limbed, rakish moves added to his 'lost boy' air. Even in the perfectly tailored suit, there was a wildness about him that seemingly fascinated everyone. But not her. She would never succumb to those looks— the grumpiness and mystery he exuded was a deliberate ploy. She checked but there was nothing on the company website about him. He hid the truth from *everyone*. No wonder he didn't want her here—he couldn't hide his true self from her and he knew she wouldn't let him get away with projecting this false front.

But she *would* do a good job—just to spite him. She would get the office full and moving. She would get those shy coders in and despite her cynicism, Mia realised his employees' obvious interest in him could be useful.

What he'd said about that cruise made a lot of sense. Bruno *had* been forever reminding his wife that she didn't *have* to work while on holiday. Worse, Sante's questions about his and Dario's accident made conflicting, confusing doubts rise. Mia knew that what she remembered wasn't always a complete picture of the past. Sometimes she'd leapt to conclusions. She'd *assumed* things because she'd not had anyone close enough—who cared enough— for her to ask the truth from. And that included her brother Dario. The carefree times *Mia* remembered from when they'd lived in Capri with her mother—when they'd had picnics in the gardens and devoured leftover luxury hors d'oeuvres—had in reality been engineered by her brother Dario, who'd scavenged them from the kitchen. Mia had only figured it out when he'd let a clue slip one day in a temper. It had taken too long for her to see her mother's absences for what they really were—the neglect of a woman desperate to find pleasure however she could. Dario had always staunchly defended their mother, but eventually it had become clear how much he'd protected Mia from her neglect.

So had what she remembered about Sante also been wrong?

No. Since the accident, Dario had kept a lot to himself but *he* believed this about Sante. Yes, he was distant and wouldn't discuss it but her brother knew better than anyone how awful their father could be. So for Dario to believe the worst of Sante, then *some* of it had to be true. Even though she'd fought with Dario when he'd wanted to correct the terms of their father's will, she knew her brother had always wanted to protect her. Now she would protect him in return.

Frustrated by her distraction, she went to the swanky office kitchenette and poured a glass of filtered water. She leaned back against the counter to sip it, almost choking when Sante walked in, still looking tense. He checked his step but then headed to the coffee machine. His guard was clearly up and he was deliberately maintaining distance.

Full-of-mischief Mia couldn't resist challenging him on it.

'You worked through the night?' She studied him.

He looked annoyingly good for such lack of sleep. That tallied with his general physical perfection. As a teen he'd been tall and broad and fit. Blessed with athleticism and intelligence. It was incredibly annoying.

'You must be very tired.' She hoped he was. Because if he had inhuman stamina that would just be too much.

'Working long hours is normal for me,' he snapped dismissively.

She barely refrained from rolling her eyes at his grumpy abruptness. But he saw and she was provoked into sarcasm.

'So you feel the need to prove yourself smarter, stronger, fitter, faster?' she queried. 'In that total alpha male way of enduring discomfort and extreme suffering better than anyone?'

He sipped the scalding coffee without a wince and regarded her steadily, which made her all the more irrepressibly determined to provoke him into a response.

'Well, at the very least you must be very hungry,' she added.

She knew there was nothing in that gleaming fridge other than milk for the coffee. Replenishing it with more supplies was on the extensive list of questions she'd compiled for the boss if he ever made an appearance.

'I am,' he acknowledged with almost a whisker of a smile. 'That cannoncino you demolished earlier looked delicious.'

'Then you should go get yourself one,' she said with a sharp smile. 'Stretch your legs if you've been asleep at your desk. The fresh air might do wonders for your temperament.'

His jaw dropped.

Amused, her smile widened. 'I'm here to manage your workers in the office, not be your personal slave.'

There was a moment of silence in which Mia regretted her unruly tongue as she watched Sante's expression change from disbelief—and disapproval—to a look she didn't trust.

Was he almost *smirking*? And why was she suddenly gripped by the awful vision of being helpless in his hold? And could he read her mind? Because he looked like he could and would and so would she.

OMG. If he looked at her like *that*, she'd do *anything* he asked. When he smouldered he was horrifyingly tempting. *How* could she be remotely attracted to Sante Trovato?

'I thought you were going to create an environment in which my staff will *thrive*,' he drawled.

'Your staff, yes. I'll make other purchases for them accordingly now I know you're happy for me to.' She shot him a faux smile. 'I wouldn't make purchases without prior approval.'

'You might think you have all the answers, Mia, but know this. I don't trust you. I'll be keeping a close eye on everything you do here.'

It was a threat, not a come-on, but that wasn't how her body reacted. It was a terrible idea to provoke him, but that impishness within Mia still wouldn't be silenced.

'Go ahead and watch me all you want,' she murmured.

The atmosphere shimmered. She reminded herself that he was a callous user. He was the ruthless, money-hungry one. He was the one unworthy of *trust*. But she'd been in his presence for mere hours and her system was going haywire already.

Sante stared as colour swarmed in her cheeks and the cobalt-blue of her eyes deepened. She regretted that last, he knew. She also couldn't move. In truth, nor could he. They were locked in a moment of awareness that was completely…completely…

He blinked. He could get rid of her. Of course he could. He was still in charge for all her bluster.

She broke eye contact and cleared her throat. 'These are very nice facilities in the heart of Rome.'

He stilled, not trusting her flattery.

'Amazing that you gained such vast success without early investment.'

By *investment* he knew she meant her father's money. The money he'd never taken. Sante had *nothing* to prove. He'd long ago made it a rule not to give a damn what anyone thought and he deliberately kept people at a distance. Their judgement was always instant and always negative, especially if they learned anything about his past—but ultimately he couldn't care less. Mia Lorenti wasn't going to accept the truth so he wouldn't be bothered even beginning to explain. He wouldn't justify. But her very blue eyes drilled into him with an almost insolent challenge.

'I worked hard,' he muttered.

'Really,' she said. 'To go from school dropout to tech tycoon in a decade is pretty unbelievable.'

And she clearly didn't believe he had. She thought he'd cheated. Yet, here *she* was, the one working an assortment of jobs that she didn't stick at for long. She'd had the privilege of an aristocratic upbringing whereas he'd come from literally nothing and no one.

The one time he thought he'd gotten a break it had blown up in his face. He'd left the UK straight after the accident. He'd walked out of school without completing the year, forfeiting the university scholarship before they could rescind the offer. Her father had made it clear that would happen. The police might not have reason to charge him, but Lorenti had contacts and influence in other spheres.

He'd returned to the place he'd been found. Sicily. He'd worked days on the dock as a labourer—picked up any shifts he could until he could afford his own computer. Then he'd worked on his app through the night. The hours he'd put in were insane. He'd gotten interest—yes, investment— that had been *earned*. But he'd retained control.

'You're very humble,' she added, still saccharinely pointed. 'You don't ever want to brag about how you made it?'

Her interest wasn't a compliment; she angled more as if there were something dubious about his achievements.

Sante flexed his shoulders. 'No.'

'But so many people would be curious, hoping to em- ulate your success.'

'Are you asking me for career tips?' he mocked. 'I can understand your curiosity given you flit from one thing to another so frequently. Is there a reason for *your* lack of reliability?'

That heat in her eyes flared. 'Don't you even want in- dustry recognition?' She ignored his dig. 'Or is it that you prefer no recognition at all?'

'I have nothing to hide, Mia,' he said tightly. 'And I definitely don't need accolades from anyone.'

He didn't need *anything* from anyone. He certainly didn't need her needling him in this way.

'You don't care what anyone thinks?'

'I don't.' He definitely didn't care about *her* opinion. She was a snob. But somehow, she was closer. Somehow, this was more intense. Somehow, she was the only person in the world.

'You just do what you want,' she breathed.

'Yes.' His mouth dried and he could barely whisper.

'Wow.' She slowly shook her head. 'You have done well for yourself.'

Yet, she made it sound as if his hard-earned liberty were a *crime*. She had no idea the hours he'd worked, the sacrifices he'd made, to ensure his independence.

'Yes,' he repeated huskily. 'And *no one* will ever take it away from me.'

What he had now wasn't bad for an unwanted foundling who'd been bounced from foster home to foster home.

Fury flashed in her eyes but it was nothing on his.

It was bad enough that she was Dario Lorenti's sister. He avoided her brother as much as possible—while their fields had once intersected, Sante's interests were far broader than the fintech space now. His office mostly managed his property portfolio. The coders were a side project—working on the ideas he didn't have the time to dive into.

Mia's presence forced him to remember a time he'd rather forget. The culmination of a series of complete disappointments. Being blamed. Being kicked out. Alone again. She had no idea. Screw her judgement and her questions. He'd had to shut her down when she'd mentioned seeing him at the hospital. He'd been so tired by the time he'd made it there. Mia had just told him that Dario was still in surgery when her father had appeared. The bastard had ignored her because of course he'd wanted to berate Sante. But maybe ignoring her had been normal for the jerk. That would track with everything Sante knew of the guy. Dario certainly hadn't been close to the man at the time, and why was Sante wasting his time now dwelling on this?

Because the level of distraction Mia brought him was outrageous what with her blue eyes and Botticelli beautiful body. He needed more than coffee to sort his head out. That he even gave a damn was shocking enough, but the thought that she'd just looked at him with heat other than anger—

Was only because of his lack of sleep. He would *never* cross the line with an employee. Furthermore, she was a Lorenti and *he* knew what ran in her blood—selfishness, greed, betrayal...*snobbishness*. But he was sure she *had* looked at him like an absolute temptress. One minute she was ice, next moment fire and he needed space to recover.

He stalked out of the office. He'd go one better than a measly pastry; he'd have a long, leisurely lunch—*alone*.

Her eyes gleamed as she watched him walk in early the next day. 'Twice in the one week?' She shot him another saccharine smile.

'I told you I'll be watching you,' he answered abruptly.

'I wasn't sure given you just disappeared yesterday, and of course there's nothing on your schedule.' She shrugged airily. 'But the team will be delighted.'

She obviously was not. Yet, he found himself staring at her. Again. Reading those mixed messages—she was sharply acidic while smiling radiantly, and her gorgeous eyes gleamed.

Sante made the mistake of not closing his office door, which meant not only could he hear her, he could also *see* her. There was no getting away from her when he *really* needed to.

She was on a conference call to the coding team. He knew she was keeping track of them via the project management software but daily personal calls made the difference—well, that was what Adele always said and she'd clearly trained Mia to follow the routine. So why it bothered him now, he didn't know. But Mia was wildly different from Adele. Her voice carried—with its sing-song higher pitch, laced with laughter as she threatened to set a timer on for someone. She radiated a boundless joie de vivre that was extremely irritating. He heard a ripple of soft laughter and then finally there was blessed silence. Until she started humming. Then stopped. Then hummed a little again before she obviously got absorbed in her work.

Sante sat, *his* ability to concentrate obliterated. Restless after less than five minutes, he rose. Hovering at his doorway, he watched her work, intently focused on her screen. He found himself walking to her before thinking, so when she suddenly looked up into his eyes with an intensely attentive expression, he was forced to improvise.

'I'm expecting a package of documents to be delivered this week,' he said shortly. 'It's essential I get them as soon as they arrive.'

'Of course,' she replied smoothly but a deep colour ran into her creamy complexion. 'Are they late? Do you want to tell me where they're coming from and I can make contact and chase up the courier company if necessary?'

Her immediate efficiency only aggravated him more. As for that uncontrollable blush—it made *his* temperature rise. 'It's confidential.'

'Naturally.' She swallowed. 'Then I'll keep a sharp eye out and bring it to you immediately.'

Sharp eyes were definitely what she had. For a moment he gazed right into their beautiful blue. Satisfaction rippled; he liked having her full focus on him, liked seeing the pink in her cheeks deepen. Until she glanced beyond him and a sudden broad smile illuminated her face. Sante still stared, powerless to do anything but watch as she blossomed with a vitality that was extremely *alluring* and not directed at him at all.

'So nice to see you, Valerio,' she called softly.

Softly. Not the vivacious volume with which she usually spoke. Sante glanced behind him. The new graphics intern almost smiled as he avoided both Sante's and Mia's eyes entirely as he went to his desk. Sante turned back to Mia. She looked surprisingly pleased to see the jeans-and-headphones-wearing guy; her smile had turned almost intimate.

She'd been here almost two full weeks already. She knew his staff. Had she formed *relationships* with those staff—with this young kid who wasn't even on a permanent contract? But then, nor was she. Maybe they'd bonded over that. Which was fine. Naturally. Yet, he was absurdly sensitive to the different receptions she'd given him and Valerio.

Sante stalked back into his office. He jerked his chair forward, determined to focus and finally achieve *something.* But his computer suddenly pinged with a never-ending series of notifications. He went to it and frowned, staring at the calendar with consternation. He didn't pick up his phone. All patience lost, he simply hollered. '*Mia!*'

* * *

Mia drew on a defensive smile and headed into Sante's office—leaving his door wide-open behind her and trying to steady her heartbeat. Appallingly, her body responded with increasing chaos to his proximity. It didn't seem to care that he was a heartless jerk who'd betrayed her brother; her body just wanted his near. So she was ignoring her body. Controlling it.

'You've screwed up my scheduling.' He glared at her. 'Where?'

He jabbed a finger at the screen and she was forced to round his desk to study it. Big mistake. There was nowhere near enough of a barrier between them, and she desperately needed to calm her overexcited response.

'You've blocked out a significant portion of my day tomorrow.'

She leaned closer just as he turned his head towards her, meaning his mouth was only inches from hers. It was *searingly* intimate. It would take nothing to lower hers and—

What the hell was she thinking? Why had the idea to kiss him popped into her head? She stared into his brown eyes for three seconds too long.

'That's not a screw-up.' Breathless, she straightened and stepped back. 'It's a lunch meeting.'

If it weren't for Adele she would stalk out of here and not come back.

Was she coming down with some bug? Because Mia did not mix business and pleasure. She'd done that once and never would again.

'You expect me to have lunch with my employees for two and a half hours?'

Sante looked so appalled Mia had to bite back her smile.

'Not only are you going to have lunch with them,' she said. 'You're going to pay for it.'

'Why would I want to do that?'

'If you want them to come into the office more often, you need to tempt them.'

Tempt. The word hung in the air. She glanced again at his beautiful eyes in time to see *his* focus drop to her lips. They actually tingled in response. She deliberately drew a breath but got a hint of sandalwood instead of the sanity she desperately needed. His soap. It reminded her of his fresh-from-the-shower look, and now her fingers itched as much as her bones ached. For *touch*. She had to have a fever. She *hated* this guy.

'Their pay packet isn't enough motivation?' he drawled softly.

'No. You know they're all super talented. They're capable of getting money elsewhere. They need something a little more special.'

'This is your amazing action plan? What *more special* do you have in mind?'

'Time with you.'

'*I'm* the special temptation?'

'Absolutely.' She couldn't bear to look at him anymore. She dropped her gaze and stepped back, clearing her throat. 'And some food will get them over the line.'

'You're serving me up as the centrepiece of your feast?'

She stifled a chuckle because he was so very appalled as he asked. And the image it put in her mind was irresistible.

'It's a lunch session with you, so yes.' She swallowed.

'They want to work for you. They're inspired by you. *You* are the draw.'

He followed her to the door. 'Is that why you're here— because of me?'

That stopped her. She turned to face him. 'We both know I didn't know you were you when I said yes to Adele. *Adele* is my special reason.'

He glanced past her out to the open-plan office, then back to meet her eyes. 'I have to maintain distance between my employees. I'm not there to be their best friend or... anything.'

Mia suddenly flushed with heat. Did he think he was letting her down gently? Making the boundaries very clear? Had he read her mind earlier? She was mortified. And mad. Because *he* was the one looking at her with that edge of inappropriate interest. She hadn't—wasn't— *wouldn't*. And mortified, mad Mia invariably said things she shouldn't. 'You don't think you can have friends in the workplace?'

It was the way she said it that was off. Unintention- ally intimate.

'I don't think any kinds of relationships in the work- place are wise.'

Oh, he was definitely warning her but he definitely didn't need to. She'd already made that mistake with the one relationship she'd actually had and while she'd made many mistakes in her life, she didn't *repeat* the same ones. The public humiliation of that affair had burned com- mon sense into her. Hadn't it? But she simply refused to agree with Sante on this. She squared her shoulders. 'I disagree—'

'Naturally,' he muttered.

She glinted. 'Surely, even you have to acknowledge that employee satisfaction matters.'

And he needed to work on his own boundaries because he'd been the one looking at her in a way that was… just like the way he was looking at her now. *Like he was hungry.*

'Satisfaction?' he echoed.

This time it was the way that *he* said it that was off. Unintentionally intimate. It *had* to be unintentional. She bit her lip.

'What about my satisfaction?' he murmured.

'Your…?'

'What's in it for me?' he clarified.

Mia's irritation mushroomed. Of course there had to be something in it for him. He might not have taken her father's money, but he was still only about himself.

'Increased employee productivity,' she snapped. 'They'll make you more money.'

'I don't need to make more money,' he said coolly but his eyes glinted. 'I can't spend the money I earn from interest alone.'

'Well, you've brought these people together for *some* reason,' she argued, irritated. 'Don't you want them to reach their full potential?'

Otherwise, why did he have them here? If he was ludicrously wealthy, what goal did he have in mind for this group of baby geniuses?

'They're here for you so why not try it this once and see what happens? If it's a failure, then you've your first reason to fire me. What have you got to lose?'

He gazed right into her eyes. 'So when this proves

pointless, it's one strike against you.' He nodded. 'You know you only get three.'

'One week, three strikes, you're watching me, I get it.' She rolled her eyes. 'You can't wait for me to fail. Your problem is I'm not going to.'

'No?'

'No. And while we're negotiating, I suggest you have an open-door policy whenever you're actually in the office.'

'A *what*?'

'So you're more approachable.'

'*Why* would I want to be more approachable?' He looked as irritated as she felt. 'I just said relationships in the workplace are—'

'You come across as very intimidating,' she interrupted.

'And that's a negative?'

'When you want the best from your staff, yes. Don't you want them to feel confident enough to toss their creative ideas about without feeling terrified of your reaction?'

'What makes you think they're *terrified*? You've barely seen me with them.' His eyes narrowed when she abruptly laughed.

'Because you're barely here.' She shook her head.

'So you think they require more of my involvement.'

'Inspiration,' she corrected.

Terrified had been too strong a word; they were nervous. They all wanted to *please* him.

'They idolise you,' she acknowledged, her voice oddly husky. 'They want to be you.'

Sante didn't preen. Didn't appear flattered in any way. If anything, he looked angrier.

'They idolise and want my *bank balance*. That's all.'

Two days ago she would've agreed it was his single-minded stratospheric success they wanted to emulate. But the team he'd assembled out there seemed to be as excited about *him* as much as the opportunity to earn money. They were turning up again right now because Valerio had just put out the word that Sante was back in the office again. And they were all smiling about it. And if Sante had really achieved all this success *without* her father's start-up funding, then she could understand why. She was outrageously curious about him; of course they were, too. They wanted to learn from him. But Sante's unwillingness to believe that was weird.

'Perhaps you underestimate what you have to offer,' she said.

He didn't move but that stark, almost lost, expression flared in his eyes. It was the briefest moment, a flash of vulnerability she never would believe if she'd not just seen it. A wave of temptation washed over her—that inappropriate ache to move nearer to him. The man had a *lot* to offer—physically at least, and she was losing her mind because when she looked into his eyes like this, it was as if the world faded. As if there were only them and only—

'Fine.' He suddenly turned away from her. 'I'll be at your meeting.'

CHAPTER FOUR

SANTE GLANCED AT the clock in the corner of his screen and grimaced. He didn't want this meeting but he *had* been absent from the office a lot. He should've scheduled it himself, controlled the environment more. Excluded her. Because the open-door thing was the worst ever. He'd end that little experiment immediately. As a safety net for keeping his interactions with her appropriate, it was a complete fail. When he caught sight or sound of her, he forgot anyone else, anything else, existed. She was fascinating and it was a constant source of frustration because he did not want to be *fixated*. He rose and walked to close the door just in time to watch her walk across the foyer carrying a platter to the boardroom.

She glanced up and caught him staring. She paused. No point pretending he wasn't watching her. He'd warned her he would, so he was justified—yes? But though he should look away, close the door, he couldn't. He was trapped. A slow blush mottled every inch of the creamy skin he could see. Her eyes widened and her lips parted—suspended in that moment of surprise. She was almost a statue were it not for the thrum of her blood giving her away. Undeniable awareness captured them *both*.

With brute strength Sante closed the door. Closed his

eyes. Focused on drawing a breath. Mia Lorenti was driving him *insane*. She sounded cool, looked professional, was doing everything perfectly well. But every so often that heat flashed in her eyes and she spoke with a huskiness that made every muscle within him tighten in sensual response. His instincts sharpened, too. He'd think she was playing him if it weren't for the fact that the blushes like that one just now were too awkward, too uncontrollable. They *couldn't* be deliberate. She tried to stop physically reacting to him but couldn't seem to. A feeling he knew well.

He paced in his office but it wasn't large enough to burn the excess energy. He yanked the door open again and stalked out—almost colliding with her on her way back to the kitchenette in the process. Automatically, he reached out, steadying her. That brought him far too close—he caught her fresh citrus scent laced with pastry cream sweetness. He dropped his hands as if he'd been scalded. But he didn't step back. He couldn't. He was frozen.

'Sante?'

He couldn't stand that whisper. Nor that soft inquiry in her eyes. He made himself glance beyond her. There were so many people milling about in the office. Truthfully, he didn't remember hiring them all—or had Adele been on a bigger hiring spree while he'd been travelling? He shook his head, knowing she hadn't. He'd just been distracted with his last property deal, hence his prolonged absence. While he kept a close eye on the programming and project files, he did that mostly from a distance and left Adele to deal with the face-to-face issues like thermostat control, supplies, illness, morale, general interaction…

'It's okay, they won't bite,' Mia murmured.

He glanced back and was immediately lost in the inviting generosity of her looks—the depth of those blue eyes, the endless creaminess of her skin. She was bone-achingly luscious.

Indeed, *he* was the one tempted to *bite*. 'I'm going for a walk,' he muttered, constricted.

'But—'

Getting away from her was imperative. He jogged down the stairs out into the spring day, soon enveloped by throngs of tourists. He would remind himself *exactly* who was boss. That he could do this. He'd dealt with far worse than a damned meeting with his own team. He huffed out several deep breaths. He was fine. This was fine. This was nothing.

He made it back with only a couple minutes to spare. She was hovering outside the boardroom door, her eyes overbright and alert, and he wished he had the strength to look away from her.

'For a moment there I thought you weren't going to show,' she murmured.

Uh-huh, so had he. But he wasn't going to confirm her worst opinions of him.

He glanced in at the boardroom. Half the team was seated already and emanating a hum of conversation that covered the too-intense conversation he was having with her. Sante's stomach rumbled at the sight of the spread on the back table. An assortment of pastries was in a pile at the farthest end—including some of the cream ones she'd eaten the other day. But he was forced to enter if he wanted one. And he *really* wanted one. So did everyone else. Of course she hadn't done this just for him. She'd done this for everyone.

'You're spoiling them,' he muttered.

Mia looked right into his eyes. 'Doesn't everyone deserve to be spoilt occasionally?'

How was it possible she could sound so cool yet her gaze be so hot? She was a complete contradiction. Seemingly so controlled yet on the verge of combustion at the same time. Or maybe he was projecting his own feelings. Energy surged within him again. That walk had been pointless. How was he supposed to make idle chat with his employees when all he wanted was to look at *her*? When all he wanted was to lose himself in the soft generosity of her form?

'You won't be attending the session,' he clarified crisply.

'No.' That light in her eyes dimmed and her flush deepened. 'I'll pop in only to ensure everyone has everything they need.'

'Good.' He couldn't concentrate when she was around.

Mia hid at the back of the boardroom and tried not to let her hurt anger show. Tried not to watch Sante too obviously. As she'd expected, every one of his coders and creatives had turned up. She'd worked so hard trying to ensure everyone had comfort and space. She'd sourced pastries from her favourite bakery, balanced them out with salads and fresh fruit, but while the spread was sensational, it was clearly Sante himself who was the draw. Just as she'd known he would be. Not that he looked at all pleased about it. Not that he even wanted her in the room. Which was rude enough, and couldn't the guy manage the smallest smile of welcome to his baby geniuses? He put a pastry on the plate he'd taken and turned, encountering her frank stare. He turned to stone. She shot him a wide smile back, damned if she was going to let him know he'd killed her mood. He blinked. Broke eye contact. Frowned harder.

The room was so packed she left the door open so air could circulate freely. So she could eavesdrop. Given the glass and light, she could already see him.

It wasn't a straightforward meeting from the start. There was no round-up of where projects were at, like the calls she made at the start of each day. He just went straight to it.

'What are the problems?'

Momentary silence. Then Sante glanced to his left. 'Davide? What's the issue stopping the pop-app development?'

Davide coughed, coloured then admitted he had no idea.

'Good,' Sante answered. 'Honesty is good. So let's break it down.'

He clicked to project a file on the large screen. To the right of the code, Mia saw the chat list full of suggestions. Comments from the username 'S' were plastered down the field. The guy mightn't be in the office much but he was all over their files. He hadn't needed the catch-up; he already knew each project inside and out.

Mia didn't catch what someone said but Sante went very still for a moment before suddenly bursting into an explanation, almost frenzied in speed and detail. He paced, energy sparking from him, a marker in each hand, and swiftly covered the glass board behind him in incomprehensible scribble, though apparently everyone else present could both read and understand it. He was a conduit for electricity; the atmosphere in the room surged with energy. Everyone leaned forward, fully focused and hanging on his every word—and there were so many words tumbling from him with speed until they suddenly spaced out into nothing as his brain raced too far ahead of his tongue. Everyone else simply tried to catch up while he amended the mess on the board with more scribble but in another colour. Fascinated, Mia slipped in the back of the room to watch the frenzy of question, answer, deeper explanation—almost none of which she understood.

'The guy's a machine,' one of the coders near Mia muttered. 'I don't know how he does it.'

'Another level entirely,' the guy seated in front of her agreed.

It went for far longer than she'd put in the damned schedule. As Mia replenished the snacks and brought in fresh coffee, she finally realised the disconcerting truth. This disparate brilliant bunch of people Sante had assembled wasn't dreaming up ideas for him to take and monetise; they were here to develop and realise the ideas *he'd* put forward to them. They were in *teams* to dissect and test all kinds of different possibilities because Sante had too many viable schemes to be able to consider fully all on his own. He mightn't appear much in the office but he made notes within their projects on the daily—he knew exactly where each of them were at without needing to ask. The man was on another level in everything— intelligence, drive, strength and yes, looks. Even with his perma-frown and distancing demeanour. She was *fascinated*. But only in the same way as his underlings; it definitely wasn't that she *wanted* him in a sexual way. But the churning feeling in her lower belly begged to differ.

And that was a huge problem. Not only was Sante her brother's enemy, he was effectively her *boss*. She backed out of the room, sternly reminding herself that the last time she'd gotten involved with someone at work she'd blown up her life.

Barely eighteen and only a few months before his untimely death, Mia had fully fallen out with her father and taken a job as a nanny. She'd loved the glimpse into a happy family life that she'd never had. Then she'd met Oliver, the young 'fun uncle' of her charges. Five years older than her, he'd told her she was everything he'd ever wanted. Which was all an attention-starved Mia had needed to hear. She'd *desperately* yearned to be loved and she was such a cliché for being the nubile young nanny who'd slept with someone in her employer's family.

Her father's jaundiced judgement of her as a party girl in high school hadn't been entirely inaccurate. She'd liked to escape school to go out dancing, but actually she'd avoided one-on-one physical intimacy. Deep down she'd been afraid her father was right. That she'd be needy and make bad choices in the heat of impulse—like her mother had.

But Oliver had been patient and persistent. He'd not just wooed her, he'd love-bombed her and eventually she'd believed him. But once she was wrapped around his little finger he'd alternated between attentive or absent. She'd tried harder to be more what he wanted. Tried not to be too much so he wouldn't get sick of her. She'd wanted him to keep wanting her. And in all that emotional angst she'd become distracted. She'd messed up at work—not majorly, but repeatedly in small ways. Until the day she'd found out—publicly—that Oliver had a serious girlfriend. He'd just been using Mia.

She'd been mortified when the housekeeper had watched her exposure with patronising derision. Her colleagues had *all* known. They'd all watched her waltz into it. They'd actually taken *bets* as to whether it would be the father or the brother who had her. When she'd confronted Oliver he'd actually laughed. Was she *serious*? Oh, he would sleep with her but he'd never settle with someone like *her*. She'd left the job that day, her confidence so obliterated she'd avoided intimacy since, choosing to prove to herself that she was capable of working hard and not wrecking her own future by acting on emotional impulse or desire. Now she knew—mixing business with pleasure always ended in a mess. So she was going to do a good job here and now. She would *not* screw up. That meant not screwing with Sante in *any* way. That also meant not staring at him like he was the most beautiful man she'd ever seen—even though he was. She would maintain her professionalism. And she would not provoke him about the past—because she was beginning to wonder whether she didn't know as much about all that as she'd thought she had.

But she never should have suggested Sante leave his office door open. Now she heard him actually laughing and felt stupidly wounded when he didn't treat her the way he did the coders or the legal and accounting staff. And now—at the end of the meeting—he discovered that she'd established an inter-office league with a 'game of the week.' She'd set up a gaming console in the far corner of the office with a couple of controllers, and to her amazement he'd added his name to the property division team and was helping them—*her* team—catch up to the coders' tally before the end of day and it was…too *okay* of him when she needed him to remain a villain. When she needed to stop herself slipping beneath his spell.

When she'd worked on board the cruise liners she'd always rolled her eyes at the guys who'd leered at her. The ones who'd told her they'd taken one look and wanted her. Now *she* was that guy. Driven by hormones and basic instinct. The physical yearning she felt was almost unbearable. It was lust at first look and it was only getting worse. This was different to her experience with Oliver—that had been slow burn and flattery until he'd flipped on her. *Her* reaction to Sante was too strong, too all-consuming. But she could and would shake it off. Except she was parked outside his office nine hours a day. And he was inside it. Constantly.

She glowered first thing Thursday morning when she got in early as usual and saw him lodged in place at his desk.

'You slept in the office again, didn't you?' she said accusingly.

While his suit was fresh and his hair damp and more unruly than ever, he had a burning look in his eyes and his muscular frame was tense. Was he tired after yesterday? She understood the man had introvert tendencies; had it been too much? In which case, why was he still here?

'Why do you need to work all night?' she goaded. 'I thought you were so rich you couldn't possibly spend it all.'

'I work all night if something is so all-consuming that

I *can't* sleep until I have satisfactory resolution,' he answered huskily.

Mia stilled, quelling her shiver. The man was *intense*. 'Okay, then have this.'

He glanced at the box she had in hand and his eyebrows arched. 'Why, Mia, are you spoiling *me*?'

'No, it's left over from the meeting yesterday,' she lied.

He pushed away from his desk and walked round to where she was frozen two steps into his office. 'And you don't want it? Are you not well?'

'No, I'm just…'

'Being sweet and putting my needs ahead of yours.'

She gaped at him. He actually thought something nice about her? She didn't trust him and she definitely needed to put distance between them. To get this irresistible magnetism under control.

'No, I'm putting your *staff* needs first, hoping this will even out your mood so we have less of the frowning. You did okay yesterday, so we don't want to ruin the progress now.'

He actually chuckled. '*We*. Wow.' He picked up the pastry, broke it and held half the resulting slightly squished mess out to her. 'Then maybe we should manage your mood, too. Share it with me.'

Mia stared at him warily. Was this a dare? Or was he serious? Serious, apparently. Because he broke it in two, clearly unconcerned about crumbs flaking everywhere. The generosity was unexpected but oddly, she wasn't surprised. She'd watched him yesterday with his coders. And she could act like an adult. So she took the piece he offered, bit into it and suppressed her moan.

'Yes.' His lips quirked. 'They really are exceptional.' He demolished his piece in the one gulp.

Of course he was the sort to simply devour what he wanted. A stray thought escaped her tight control—she wished he'd want her.

'You lied to me,' he said softly.

Startled, she blinked. 'What—'

'That pastry wasn't from yesterday.' He moved closer, his mouth curving. 'That was fresh.'

Was he *teasing* her? Mia's pulse jumped.

'You *are* spoiling me,' he added, almost smirking.

No. She was just being a decent human. Not doing anything special for *him*.

'I didn't know you were ambidextrous,' she babbled.

The corners of his eyes creased and his smile broadened ever so slightly. He was clued in on her desperate deflection. 'Yes, I'm good with both hands.'

Oh, sure. She really shouldn't but she really could imagine all kinds of things he could do with those hands.

An ache opened up within her—mingling with regret. She liked seeing him smile. Why didn't he smile more? Why didn't he tease like this a little more? It was as if she'd suddenly caught a glimpse behind a big grey wall and seen the playful Sante behind it. Why did he hide his humour? Why did he stay so distant and serious? Why was he so very alone despite all this success?

She shouldn't be so curious. She should remain professional. Keep up her resistance—because she realised now just how easily she could slip beneath his spell. But that could mean more than humiliating gossip—he was her brother's enemy, wasn't he?

'Of course you are,' she murmured, unable to resist the fire in this moment. 'You're good with everything.'

Somehow, he was closer. *She'd* stepped closer.

He shook his head and blinked and that smile faded. 'You shouldn't—'

'Sante—oh, sorry.' Paolo cleared his throat.

Mia whirled away, horrified that the lawyer had caught her standing too close to the boss. Being alone with him in his office. *She'd* been leaning in. She'd gotten too close. She'd made that mistake. Of course *she* had.

Always-makes-mistakes Mia; always-too-much Mia. And she was beginning to worry she'd made more kinds of mistakes regarding Sante than in his office just now. She felt forced to reconsider what she'd believed for so long—but he didn't want to discuss it and Dario never would, either.

Sante set his jaw, irritated as hell by his lawyer's interruption but at the same time immeasurably grateful. He'd been about to make a massive mistake—entranced by her interest and attention and proximity. But at Paolo's appearance, Mia had fled. Scarlet-cheeked. Sweet. Utterly unable to hide that responsive light in her eyes. And he was flummoxed.

He'd worked through the night again, desperate to regain his own focus, sparked by the fact he'd struggled to concentrate in the meeting yesterday—hell, he'd gone down a complete rabbit hole with a few of the coders just to pass the time safely, and then sat down and gamed with another couple of them. He hadn't gamed in years and had been rustier than he'd liked. Competitiveness had kicked in. Especially when he'd seen Mia listed as the second-highest scorer in the property team. He'd been both in-trigued and compelled to beat her score.

For a moment there this morning he'd thought he'd dreamed her up. But he'd been hanging out for her ar-rival, and her utterly unimpeachable appearance hadn't disappointed. She was amusingly determined to give him nothing to pull up. But while she was professionally, even conservatively dressed, that long skirt hugged her hips and the neat blouse was perfectly buttoned and he just wanted to—

No. He didn't want to do anything. It wasn't appropri-ate to even *think* anything. And yet, he'd seen her expres-sion light up when she saw him and then she'd offered him some of her breakfast, and any resolve he'd had evapo-rated.

And he still couldn't stop watching her. It was like the more he tried, the more impossible it became. Aside from his personal distraction, he had to admit the meeting yes-terday had gone far better than he'd expected. Mia had woven through the room a couple of times, keeping an eye on everyone's comfort. She'd gone to a lot of trouble, ensuring everyone was at ease—especially that one coder who struggled most with sensorial overwhelm and Sante had never expected to actually show up. But Mia had en-abled him to—radiating positivity, optimism, energy, en-thusiasm. She *was* like a damned nanny, getting the best out of her charges. But *Sante* did not want to be babied.

He was supposed to be listening to his lawyer now. Instead, he was locked on watching her walk back to her desk. Vibrant, voluptuous, full of vitality and slightly wild. She was the most devastatingly attractive woman he'd ever seen.

He struggled to focus on Paolo's questions. Struggled for a further two hours. He'd failed to shut his door, which meant he could hear whenever she spoke—welcoming his staff as they came in, answering their fairly frequent stupid questions. Just as he was about to go out and tell them to go do some actual work, she redirected them and got them back on task. She was annoyingly good at managing them and they clearly liked her. Excess energy coiled within him, making his skin tight and his resistance weak.

He could get his self-control back. He just needed occupation. He'd wanted to prove to himself that he still had it. That he wasn't thinking about her all the time. But it was barely an hour before he gave in and stalked out to her desk.

'No sign of that delivery yet?'

She didn't look up, just shook her head. 'You'd have it if it had arrived. I know you're waiting for it.'

Right, he'd been out too often to ask. But he hesitated, unable to walk away.

'I promise I'll bring it to you as soon as it arrives.' She finally glanced up.

He gazed into her soft eyes and realised that she *was* managing him, too. Ensuring he had food, coffee, communicating clearly to temper his expectations. The realisation annoyed the hell out of him.

How was he reduced to asking about a set of plans that he didn't care all that much about? It was a flimsy excuse to engage with her. He was *pathetic*. He'd done too many all-nighters over the years because he was clearly losing his ability to bounce back and redirect his brain. It was stuck on the one track. He just wanted to be near her. It didn't matter that he was playing with fire; he *saw* the awareness in her eyes. He *knew* she felt it, too. That only made it worse. But he was her boss and he wasn't going to be this weak. Why would he be such a fool to get involved with a Lorenti?

But Mia wasn't like her father, nor her brother. She was far more open. Far more generous with her laughter and warmth.

Screw 'being seen in the office.' He'd been present more this week than he had almost all year. His team was great—on fire, in fact, working hard. They didn't need him. What *he* needed was a break from everything. Especially her. *Immediately.*

CHAPTER FIVE

Just before midday on Friday, Mia frowned at the thick envelope and double-checked the sender's details. This was definitely the package Sante had been waiting on—he'd been at her desk every thirty minutes or less every day this week demanding an update. Now it was finally here but *he* wasn't here to receive it. She glanced at his office but he hadn't materialised in the three minutes since she'd last looked. Her irritation levels escalated. She checked the meeting schedule but there was nothing blocked out in there for him—although he didn't ever fill it in. She phoned him but yet again, it went straight to voice mail. He'd not yet replied to her earlier email, either. She drummed her fingers on the desk and tried not to worry. She would focus on another task. He would turn up or phone in soon enough.

Two hours later he'd done neither of those things. The parcel preyed on her mind—he'd *really* wanted it. But if he wasn't going to bother telling her where he was, then she couldn't courier it to him directly, could she? Bracing, she walked to the lawyer's office.

'Paolo, do you know where Sante is today?'

Paolo glanced up from his computer. 'No, but I'm not

surprised if he doesn't show. He's been abnormally present this week.'

Yeah, there were reasons for that. 'Do you know where he's likely to be?'

Paolo's gaze drifted back to his screen, clearly unfazed. 'If he's not answering calls he's probably offline.'

No kidding, Sherlock.

'And where would offline be in Sante's world?' Mia summoned patience. 'I just want to courier a parcel to him.'

He'd said he was going to keep a close eye on her. Now he wasn't here and he'd not bothered to tell her where he was or why, which didn't track given the complete lack of distrust he had over everything she did. But it was Friday, the end of her 'week' and what if this was a test? Sante wanted this document delivered immediately but maybe he'd removed himself to an impossible location to confound her. Just when she'd thought they'd almost reached a cordial working relationship, when she was starting to think he wasn't entirely as awful as she'd long believed. Well, she wasn't failing and he wasn't winning.

'If he's not at his Rome apartment, he'll most likely be at the Sicilian estate,' Paolo muttered. 'Courier won't deliver there before Wednesday at the earliest. You could scan and email the contents.'

There was no way she was opening this envelope. It had 'private and confidential' stamped all over it. 'Can I get the address for both? I'll find a way to get the hard copy to him.'

Paolo clicked a few times and jerked his chin towards the printer. 'If he's not in Sicily, then it could be any of the others on the list.'

Mia gaped at the list of properties that emerged from the printer. Aside from the Sicilian and Rome addresses, there were places in Paris, Madrid, New York—there was even a property in Melbourne, Australia. She was hardly going to circumnavigate the globe to get this to him, but she would at least try the first couple given he'd been banging on about it for days. She would prove herself to Sante Trovato. Because his unexplained absence was aggravating. If she didn't know he regularly went *offline* she might actually worry about him. Okay, she *was* worried about him. He'd worked through the night too many times this week and he'd seemed particularly ragged by the end of day yesterday. What if he was unwell? Surely, all that lack of sleep had to catch up to him at some point.

Mia set an auto-response on her email, picked up the package and set forth. More than eight hours later she stiffly got out of the taxi and stretched out her cramping muscles. She'd gotten no reply when she'd buzzed the door at the Rome apartment, so she'd gone to the airport. Despite her frequent attempts, he'd still not picked up so she'd flown to Palermo and then struggled to find a driver willing to drive her *all* the way here. The trip had taken way more time and effort than she'd expected. Now she stared at the enormous stone wall that obscured any view of the house and garden. It wasn't exactly inviting.

'Do you mind waiting?' she asked the driver.

He immediately frowned.

'I'll be as quick as I can.'

The gigantic gates were firmly closed but the pedestrian gate on the left was slightly ajar. She would hand the wretched package to Sante, turn around, walk out to face another long drive, flight and taxi before finally getting home. She didn't care about working all the hours or proving anything anymore. She just wanted this over.

She trudged up the winding tree-lined driveway wishing she had better shoes than her office pumps. Was this even the right address? That stone wall was deceptive—tall and bland, it shielded a seemingly endless expanse of palm trees, wide stretching lawns, an ornamental lake, even a citrus grove. Between the trees she glimpsed an enormous iron greenhouse and realised it was a vast private paradise. She steeled herself against its beauty but she was reminded of Palazzo di Constanzo, the estate her father had bought to house her mother in Capri after he'd walked out on their marriage when Mia was only a baby. Mia had spent the first few years of her life there—swimming and playing in an enormous garden like this only more neglected, more wild. Nostalgia hit. She'd had a freedom there that she'd never really had since. One she knew Dario missed, too—he'd loved their home in Capri. And she understood how this place would fit Sante—it was a stunning sanctuary in which a lone wolf could freely roam.

Turning the corner she saw the main building and she stopped. It wasn't like the beautiful villas she'd seen on the journey here; it was an enormous palazzo—an imposing structure far too large for a single occupant. The lone wolf ought to have an entire pack.

Finally, she made it to the enormous front door. There would be staff here. The property was too sprawling and too perfect not to be tended by an army of housekeepers and gardeners. She would give the parcel to the first staff member she saw and escape without even having to face Sante. Good.

Brushing her hair from her hot face, she rang the bell. It pealed loudly, echoing long after she'd released the button. Her confidence faltered as no footsteps sounded inside. As no one answered. Steeling herself, she pressed the button again. If Sante wasn't here, she was going to throttle him the next time she—

'Mia?' A harsh voice snapped behind her. 'What are you doing here?'

Mia spun. Sante was standing at the foot of the stairs behind her. She stared, so startled her heart stopped. He was wearing faded shorts, heavy boots and nothing else. Why wasn't he wearing anything else? Why was he sweating? And how had she not heard him walking with heavy boots like those?

'Mia?' he repeated, clearly irritated. 'Why are you *here*?'

He sounded furious but he looked so outrageously earthy, she just snapped right back.

'Why aren't you wearing a shirt?' She clutched the package to her chest and glared at him angrily. 'You should be wearing a shirt!'

'In my own garden?' He stomped up the stairs to glare at her directly in the eyes. 'When I wasn't expecting guests?'

'I'm not a guest,' she argued. 'I'm…'

Fully distracted. He was strong, vital, *physical*—about as man as a man got—oozing testosterone and power. Dirt was smeared on his legs and forearms and the next second his forehead as well as he swept a hand through his already messy hair. As he moved, his muscles rippled. Mia gaped at his abs, his gleaming chest, his broad shoulders. She couldn't drag her gaze away as he stepped nearer and took up all her visual space.

'What do you want?' he repeated huskily.

Utterly thrown by the expanse of bronzed skin and flexing muscles, Mia couldn't think let alone keep her emotions in check. 'What do I *want*? I want you to answer your damned phone.'

'What?' He patted his pocket and frowned. 'Why?'

Yeah, it was obvious he didn't have his phone on him. He had barely *anything* on him.

'So I could tell you this had finally arrived.' She held out the package to him.

An astounded expression widened his eyes. 'You came all the way to Sicily to deliver mail?'

There was grumpy and there was rude, and this was both with his thunderous frown as bonus.

'Given you've spent all week asking me five times a day whether it had arrived, I assumed it was vitally important!' She tossed the package at his feet with a thud. 'So you could at least show a little gratitude. But no, your true colours emerge. You might not have taken my dad's money but you're still a selfish jerk who doesn't care about inconveniencing everyone else.'

She was *pissed*. How dare he be here looking all relaxed and living his best outdoor life and not giving her or anyone else a second thought? And she was doubly pissed with herself for responding to him on such a basic level. Her hormones were activated—it was a raw sexual attraction to the most wildly inappropriate man ever. One who clearly couldn't think of anything worse than *her* appearing on his doorstep unexpectedly.

'How did you even get here?' He ignored her outburst.

'Taxi, plane, taxi,' she shot.

'*Commercial* plane?' He looked at her like she was insane. 'Why didn't you take the helicopter?'

Her jaw dropped. 'As if I would just use an expensive resource without authorisation.'

He sucked in a deep breath and glanced heavenward as if summoning patience. 'I see why you and Adele get on so well,' he sneered. 'By the time I recompense all your travel fees, it'll work out around the same. The last taxi alone—'

'You weren't around for me to ask,' she interrupted, not wanting to think about what the running tab must be on that taxi by now. 'If you'd bothered to answer your phone, then you could have told me that the stupid thing isn't that important and I'd have just left it on your desk for the next time you felt like cos-playing CEO.'

A startled look entered his eyes, then he laughed. Which shocked Mia all over again. She stared—hit by his appalling gorgeousness. When he laughed he was all perfect teeth, bunched muscles, gleaming eyes and sexy-as-hell tousled hair—

It was the last straw. She'd busted her gut to get this stupid package to him and he didn't give a damn. He hadn't snatched it up and torn it open like she'd expected. He simply didn't care. *All* her effort had been a complete waste of time.

Speechless, she stomped down the stairs and began the route march down the infuriatingly long driveway. His lack of gratitude—or even interest—was humiliating. She wasn't staying a second longer. She'd truly thought she'd been doing the right thing but why had she wanted to do a good job for *him*?

'Mia.'

Yeah, no, she wasn't listening to anything he had to say. She was getting back to that exorbitantly expensive taxi, which was only that expensive because his ridiculously beautiful palazzo was miles away from anywhere so everything about this mess was all *his* fault. She bit the inside of her lip, holding back her vitriolic mutter because the driveway was long and she had a hotspot on the back of her heel that was going to be a blister any moment and she *hated* him.

'Mia!'

The day truly couldn't get worse. That driver better still be waiting—

'Mia!' Sante grabbed her arm and stopped her by way of standing right in front of her.

Which meant she got another eyeful of his beautiful body. She forced herself to glare at the tree to the left of him. 'I've not got time to talk. I've got a plane to catch.'

'No, you don't.'

'You can't stop me.'

'Maybe *I* can't,' he huffed. 'But a storm can.'

'What storm?' There was no storm, it was hot and—

'Looked up lately?'

No, she could barely look away from his stunning form. She met his fiery gaze just as a fat raindrop hit her arm. She glanced at it just as another landed. Then another. Okay, the day could get *much* worse. Rain like this was going to soak her in seconds. Glancing up she saw dark grey and deep purple clouds rapidly descending.

'That's why I was outside securing anything that can move. There's going to be high wind, heavy rain, power outages. It's not safe to be out—'

'I'm not going to be,' she growled. 'I'm getting my

taxi.' But though she rose on tiptoe, she couldn't see the car waiting on the other side of those gates.

'He'd have left the moment he dropped you,' Sante advised bluntly. 'He'd have seen the clouds and fled. It's hitting sooner than they forecast.'

'I'll be fine.' She was not going back to that palazzo with him. Only now the rain hit harder.

'You're going to walk fifty kilometres to the nearest village?' he asked sarcastically. 'You need to come inside.'

No. But the wind lifted and the tumbling rain became more than torrential.

He gestured impatiently at the rapidly darkening sky. 'How wet do you want to get?'

'I'm *not* going to your house.'

'Too bad. We don't have time to argue.' He suddenly launched forward, grabbing her low and so hard her shriek was knocked from her chest before she could release it. Next thing she knew she was upside down over his shoulder and it was—

'What are you *doing*?' she yelled, even though it was ridiculously obvious. 'Put me down!'

'No.' He tightened his arm around the backs of her thighs and actually sounded happy. 'You probably have blisters from walking up the drive in those shoes already.'

She wasn't admitting to that. 'I'm too heavy for you to carry all the way to the house.'

'I was a dockworker for years. I think I can handle you,' he yelled back. 'You're nothing.'

She was hardly *nothing*. 'You just want to prove yourself,' she muttered—not expecting him to hear.

'That's right. It's the alpha male in me. Isn't that what

you'd say?' His burst of laughter was such a shocking sound that it silenced her.

She tried not to be mortified, tried not to like this a little too much—but she completely failed on all fronts. She had the most amazing view of his legs, not to mention an intimate appreciation of his incredible strength.

He didn't climb the steps to the grand entrance of the palazzo but went through one of the arches to the sheltered space beneath. Once there he finally bent, carefully sliding her down his body until she was back on her feet. Her skirt was wet through and so thin it slithered up as she slid down. Which meant she might as well have been naked as she was plastered against *his* heat and his near nudity.

Breathless, she gazed up at him. She was woozy from being upside down, right? Not from this hot, wet skin-to-skin contact. His body suddenly flexed and a bolt of pure electricity shot through her in response. She quaked—a mini convulsion of excitement that was way too intense and intimate for this moment. Mortified, she pushed back in the same instant he released her. Which meant she stumbled. He shot an arm around her waist again immediately.

'You okay?'

Utterly awkward, she smoothed her skirt down her thighs but it still clung to parts that really didn't need the exposure. He kept his arm around her as he opened the door and hauled her through. The furious howl of the wind and rain eased as the door slammed behind them.

Mia struggled to regain her breath. It wasn't right that she was panting when he'd been exerting all the effort.

'You can let me go now,' she mumbled.

He looked wired—more virile than ever as his muscles bunched and gleamed in the wet. For a moment she thought he was about to refuse. Instead, he inhaled deeply and stepped away from her.

Good.

Mia shivered—a belated reaction to his impact on her.

'You're cold.' He glowered.

No. She really wasn't. She reached for an alternate reason. 'That rain was crazy heavy.'

'You need to get dry.' His frown deepened as he stared at her. 'Where's your bag? Don't you have clothes?'

'I was supposed to go straight back to the airport. I'm on the last flight out.' So she only had the small purse slung over her body.

'You're not making that.' He shoved his wet hair back from his forehead and spun away from her.

'I can't stay here,' she declared.

'Not good enough accommodation?' he muttered.

'It's not the accommodation. It's the company.'

'I don't want you here, either, but we don't have much choice.'

She gritted her teeth. 'Is that package still out there getting wet?'

'I don't care.'

'I didn't drag that damn thing all the way here just for you to let it turn to pulp in a rainstorm.'

'You never needed to drag it here.'

'How was I supposed to know that when you didn't tell anyone what you were doing?'

'You know I frequently work away from the office for a few days at a stretch,' he said. 'You didn't need to come all this way just for me.'

'It wasn't for *you*,' she retorted. 'I would go the extra mile for anyone.'

She was not some lap dog leaping to please him.

'Believe it or not I just want to do a good job,' she added defensively as he glared at her. 'I have pride in my work. But you can't just disappear for days at a time,' she said, anger still getting the better of her. 'It's not fair on your people.'

'Not fair?' He looked blank. 'They know I'm fine.'

'How do they know that when you don't bother to communicate with *anyone*?'

'Because I always am.' He cocked his head. 'Track record.'

'That's not good enough,' she argued. 'Adele worries about you—'

'You bothered Adele over this?' He sounded appalled.

'Of course not. Paolo gave me a list of ten properties to try after this—'

'I don't need you to mother me, Mia. You didn't need to trouble—'

'It's not overstepping for any of us to have concerns about someone's welfare,' she argued, losing her shit entirely. 'It shouldn't be a Herculean task to let your team know where you're at. It's common courtesy!'

It wasn't okay to just disappear. Her mother had frequently disappeared from her life before her death. Her father didn't care enough to even bother. While Dario had retreated after his accident. And Oliver had gone silent in his hot and cold games. But even when there were legitimate reasons, it wasn't nice to be kept distanced from someone. *Especially* with no explanation or notice of when they might return. It was *cruel*.

Every muscle in Sante's body flexed but he suddenly stepped back. 'I'll go get the parcel.'

Alone, Mia shivered again, thrown by his rapid retreat. She needed to clear her head but her curiosity mushroomed instead. She circled, taking in the paintings covering the walls, the intricate tiled flooring, the gleaming furniture. The room was beautiful. By rights, a suite of uniformed staff ought to appear with everything she could ever want, but she had a fatalistic certainty that she was here alone with Sante.

Not good.

She wasn't an idiot; she had to stay until the storm passed, but she needed a plan to manage herself around him.

Sante reappeared in the doorway, not holding the parcel but rather a pile of clothes. 'Follow me.'

She followed, waiting a pace behind as he entered a bathroom and set the pile down before quickly backtracking and carefully avoiding her.

'You can't shower, there's lightning,' he said gruffly. 'Rub dry, get warm. There's towel, track pants, top—'

'I'm not wearing your clothes,' she muttered, mortified.

'Then go naked.' He stalked past her.

Compressing her mouth, she marched into the bathroom, closed the door and blinked at the ornate marble and gleaming fittings. It was stunning.

'Be quick,' he ordered through the door. 'Power could go out any moment.'

Yeah, no, she just had to take a moment to appreciate the sumptuous—

'*Move*, Mia.'

Could he see through walls? Grinding her teeth, she peeled her skirt and blouse off. She was sodden—including her bra and knickers, and if she left them on they would only make the dry clothes wet. So she stripped completely, hung her smalls about the room and hoped they'd dry quickly. The track pants were a little loose but such buttery soft fleece she never wanted to give them back. The merino tee was soft as well but it clung to a few curves in a way she wished it wouldn't. She stared at the mirror in horror—it was a vain hope that he wouldn't be able to tell that she wasn't wearing any underwear. Mortified, she turned away. She could be professional. She could control her unruly imagination. She could get through this.

Leaving the bathroom, she followed the faint sounds of activity, pausing in the doorway of a large but cosy lounge. Books were in piles on the shelves, more paintings, thick rugs, but it was Sante hunched by the coffee table who commanded her attention. He glanced up as she walked forward. Her breath stalled but a fireball exploded in the depths of her belly. He'd dressed in faded jeans and tee and both served to highlight his fit, muscular frame.

The lights flickered, then went out. Her breathing quickened as she heard a match strike and he lit several candles dotted on the large low table. And now the room was *far* too intimate.

'Are you hungry?' he muttered.

She was too strung out to even know, but food would *definitely* serve as a distraction. 'A snack would be great, thank you.'

He lifted the lid on a box on the table. In the flickering candlelight she glimpsed the label and struggled not to smile.

'They're from yesterday,' he said as he slid the box towards her.

'I'm sure they're still good.' She picked the smallest pastry and curled up in the nearest armchair. 'They're always good.'

Sante didn't take one. He stared at her, his scowl deepening before he rose and walked past her.

Mia stared at her pastry and tried to regulate her pulse. A soft blanket was suddenly dropped around her shoulders, cloaking her entire body.

'Thanks,' she murmured, surprised.

He sat down in the armchair opposite hers. Truthfully, she wasn't at all cold. She nibbled the pastry but it brought an assortment of associations. All of them dangerous. Desperate to ignore the temptations whispering in her head, she filled the silence. 'This place is beautiful. It must take a lot of people to maintain it.'

Sante wasn't able to speak; he could only stare. What had he done this time to be punished so cruelly? He'd come here to *escape*. Everyone. Everything. Most especially *her*. Today as he'd put furniture away and dug supports for saplings, he'd berated himself for being unable to shake his horrifying fixation on her. Then he'd heard the doorbell and walked around the house to discover he'd manifested her presence. He'd snapped simply to hide his damned delight. But she was Mia Lorenti. Adele's friend. His employee. His former friend's little sister who thought the worst of him. A rich snob to his poor boy. Utterly out of bounds.

Yet, he couldn't blame her for thinking that damned parcel was vitally important given he'd been asking her for it all day, every day. But asking about it had been an excuse to stop by her desk—he'd been getting a fix of her attention. He was *pathetic*. So he deserved to be punished by seeing her swamped in his clothing, her breasts clearly unfettered, the candlelight enhancing her radiance. Flushed and inviting, she looked as beautiful as if she'd stepped out of one of the damned frescoes that decorated the walls. He'd covered her with the blanket but he really needed to grow some self-control.

'Doesn't it?' she prompted.

Doesn't it what? He had no idea what she'd asked him; he'd been too busy drinking her in.

'No staff at all?' she added.

'No.'

He'd sent them home hours ago. Not because he was generous or anything; he'd just needed to be alone. He glanced at the window. Okay, he had wanted them to get home safely before the storm hit. He didn't want to be in any way responsible for their physical well-being. He could barely manage the damned trees, let alone the lives of others. But then Mia had appeared, inappropriately dressed for the weather, arguing with him, all at the worst possible time. The heavy clouds had swept in so quickly, it might as well be midnight.

She picked at a damned pastry and it was torment waiting for her to spill some cream on herself. He grabbed one and tore at the thing. Sometimes he still wolfed his food as if it were going to be the last meal for years so he could be a messy eater, too; and these pastries were meant for fingers and the swipe of a tongue and watching her eat them was always a sensual delight. He willed some filling to spill because he would—

'Why did you come here?' he asked abruptly, furious with himself. 'Surely, it wasn't just to deliver that parcel.'

'Yes it was,' she said stiffly. 'You were so keen to get it but then you just disappeared and when I left messages, you didn't bother getting back in touch with me.'

'So you took it upon yourself to travel all this way?'

'The last thing you said was that you'd be in first thing and then you just didn't show. You didn't even leave a message and then you didn't pick up your phone.' She glared at him.

Sante felt a discomforting guilt curl around him. She sounded like she'd been worried. There was no need for that. He was fine. Always fine. But that she'd travelled all this way?

'I flew last night,' he explained grimly. 'Turned off my phone. Left it inside today while I was out—'

'Preparing for the apocalypse,' she said acidly.

'For the storm that was forecast, yes.'

Desperate for distraction now, he picked up his phone and frowned at the mass of messages and the lack of a few specific ones. Glancing up, he saw her biting back her curiosity and couldn't help explaining. 'I've not heard from my nearest neighbours,' he said gruffly. 'They're elderly. I checked the stop bank for them but they're worried and…'

'You want to be sure they're okay. You should call them.'

He tried, but there was no answer.

'I sent my staff home first thing,' he muttered, filling the vast void. 'We'll be okay up here but if the river bursts its banks, it'll impact…'

He frowned as she lifted the blanket off her shoulders and slung it on the empty chair beside hers.

'What are you doing?' he barked.

'I'm not actually cold.'

Nor was he. And now he was back to staring at her in his favourite merino tee and he could see the curve of her breasts and her tightly budded nipples. He couldn't infer anything about her, but *he'd* never been as aroused in his life.

He desperately needed a drink. If he got blind drunk he'd effectively knock himself out. Trouble was he'd lose self-control along the way and do everything he shouldn't before becoming incapacitated. So he wasn't taking the risk. He'd stay sober. But with no power there was no television. No internet. No radio. The backup generator he had was for the fridge and for emergencies. But hell, this *was* an emergency.

He tried phoning his neighbours again, hugely relieved when they picked up. They were a distraction he desperately needed. He chatted for a while, making them promise to stay inside. 'I'll check on you as soon as the rain stops, okay?'

Finally, he ended the call and put his phone back on the table.

'Do you feel better now you know they're okay?' Mia asked with not-entirely-sweet softness.

He frowned. She might think she was making a point but he'd *needed* to be alone.

'You *can't* just disappear,' she added.

Of course he could. He'd been alone from the moment he'd been born, and he frequently disappeared. Usually, no one noticed. Certainly, no one challenged him on it.

But Mia's blue eyes flashed with more than chagrin—had she really, genuinely been concerned? He sank, lost in the blue depths. Of course she had. This was the bubbly woman who'd worked incredibly hard to welcome everyone who walked through his company doors. The caring woman who wanted his staff to make connections with each other and with him. The effervescent woman who hummed in the mornings when she thought no one was there. The woman who tried and who felt everything deeply. She sparkled and she was sweet despite her masking sarcasm. He drew in a steadying breath. She didn't deserve his anger. It wasn't her fault he had such failings. He should try to be a little more human, less beastly.

'I'm sorry I was ungracious when you arrived,' he muttered.

Her eyes widened. 'Was that—'

'An apology, yes. Savour it.'

'I will.' She slowly smiled. 'Honestly, I was starting to think the whole thing was some kind of test—so you could dismiss me sooner.'

'It wasn't a test,' he said tightly.

Her smile broadened and destroyed him—killing his ability to play nice, he simply blurted the truth. 'I didn't tell you where I was because I was trying to get away from you.'

Her face paled. 'Right. Of course.' She blinked and brushed the crumbs from her lap. 'If you could bring yourself to show me to a guest room, then you won't have to put up with my unbearable presence.'

'No. Not good enough,' he said huskily, standing the same time she did. 'I'll still know you're here. And I'll know *we're* alone.'

He watched her eyes widen, darken.

'Then what do you want me to do?' she whispered.

He moved, unable to stop advancing on her, driven to get close. 'You need me to spell it out?'

'I think so, yes.'

'I want you. I've wanted you from the second I saw you half-naked in my office. Every night I fantasise about that pastry cream—' He broke off and caught a breath. 'Actually, I fantasise about you every night and every day. Pretty much every minute.'

She slowly licked her lip. 'That must make work complicated.'

'It makes *life* extremely difficult, but I have my coping strategies.'

Her lips curved gently. 'You mean like a work-from-home day?'

'Today, right.'

'You still should have left a message.'

'I just had to get out of there,' he growled. 'It's impossible to think properly when you're in front of me.'

'Does that mean you're not thinking properly now?'

'Honestly, I'm not sure if you're even here or if I'm just dreaming.'

'You carried me up your driveway. You know I'm really here.'

Right, and his arms ached to hold her again, to place her in his bed, to arrange her so he could kiss her everywhere. 'I hoped you'd let me touch you to prove you're really here.'

'Then why not ask to touch me?'

'Because you're Mia Lorenti.'

'Mia *Simonini*—my family isn't relevant.'

He hadn't the strength to argue that one. 'I'm your boss.'

'What if *I* were to ask you to touch me?' she murmured.

He couldn't breathe. Didn't move. Didn't answer.

But she stepped closer. 'So I'd have to quit, or you'd have to fire me, before you'd consider touching me?'

'Neither of which are going to happen.' He remained still.

'But you want me.' Rampant excitement bloomed in her eyes.

Because he was damned. 'To the point of complete distraction.'

'You know technically *Adele* is my boss,' Mia said gruffly. 'She signed that contract.'

'Semantics,' he sighed. 'You know the money in your pay cheque comes from me. You know that means there's a power imbalance.'

'Not here,' she whispered. 'Not now. Here, there's only you and only me and honestly there's actually no power at all.'

CHAPTER SIX

MIA COULDN'T CLEAR the haze from her head as heat enveloped her body. Sante wanted her, but he wasn't going to *do* anything because of stupid, sane, perfectly sensible reasons. Reasons she would usually agree with but she was here and now and *her* need was too strong.

'I'm not staying,' she whispered. She never stayed anywhere for long. It was better that way. 'I'm not a permanent employee and I don't want to be. I'm only working with you because I promised Adele.'

'I know.' His voice was also barely above a whisper yet despite the incessant drumming rain, she heard him with piercing clarity as if silence had suddenly smothered the storm.

'So it's not as if there's really a conflict of interest because my being in Rome is merely a temporary thing to support someone else,' she added.

He remained rigid but she sensed his soaring energy.

'I don't want to want you, either, just so you know,' she blurted before he could deny her again. 'The fact is I'd like to end this attraction. It's not as if...'

'You'd want to bring me home to your brother.'

That struck hard. Dario *would* mind—he hated Sante,

but increasingly she wondered if Dario didn't know everything.

'He has no jurisdiction over my actions,' she said, fiercely rebelling. Sometimes her brother had the controlling tendencies of their father—though with far more loving intent. 'I'm going back to Rome tomorrow so there's only tonight. There's only us. No one else will ever know anything.' Her heart pounded as she edged closer to risk. 'You can keep a secret, right?'

His lips twisted. 'Yes.'

Oh, she liked hearing *that* word from him. But she'd screwed up before, and she needed to be sure she wasn't repeating the worst of her mistakes.

'You keep a very low profile.' She moved so close she could feel the heat, the power, thrumming within him. 'There are no pictures of you online, no info on the company website. I know that's deliberate and I don't want to invade your privacy any more than necessary, but I need to be sure you don't have a girlfriend.'

He gaped. Then growled. 'No girlfriend. I wouldn't be here with you if I did.'

He was clearly miffed but Mia didn't care about offending his moral code; she just needed certainty. 'You *swear* you're single.'

'There's *no one* in my life.' Vehemence deepened his admission, making it more desolate than he'd perhaps intended. He cleared his throat. 'Commitment isn't for me.'

'Nor me,' she muttered.

But she saw scepticism flicker immediately in his eyes. 'Don't underestimate me, Sante.'

'Underestimate you?' He edged closer, his hand

slightly brushing hers. 'You're a greater threat to me than anything.'

Yet, that fierce whisper was almost a threat in itself.

'Oh?' Her heart thundered as she tilted her head to maintain their searing eye contact.

He stared right into her soul, but his emotion—though fiery—was unreadable. Was it passion, anger, both?

'You tempt me,' he breathed raggedly. '*Terribly.*'

An overwhelming wave of pleasure washed through her, causing her raw reply to simply escape. 'Then take me.'

He was so still it was as if time had stopped. Then he moved infinitely slowly—tormenting her nerves—so very carefully closing the gap and lowering his head to hers.

Excitement rivered through her but the kiss was a feather-light graze of lip against lip—too light, too intense, too little of what she needed. He lifted, paused, his mouth a millimetre from hers—giving her one last chance to stop this. She inhaled sharply, jerkily, her lips parting in invitation, and with a full burst of excitement she rose to meet him just as he closed in again. They slammed together hard. This time their lips clung, hard and hungry; his tongue swept into her mouth and she curled hers to meet it in an immediate, hungry dance. The sensations shocked her, sending tremors throughout her body and tumbling her towards his. His growl became a groan and he clamped his arms around her waist like bands of steel. She barely noticed as he stepped backwards. She moaned in delight as his grip tightened more and more and he suddenly went down—sprawling backwards onto the large sofa, deftly lifting her in a chaotic sweep, determinedly untangling her limbs until she was across his knee and he was holding her firmly in place. She sank into his hold and tunnelled her fingers through his hair, teasing the silky mess of loose curls and dishevelment that was so very Sante.

She refused to break the kiss. Didn't care if she never breathed again and never saw another thing. Because this kiss was *everything*. She trembled with delight, needing it all—everything *now*. To be naked, to be together, to be sated—but still for this one perfect kiss to never end.

But in the end and far too soon, he broke it.

'Mia,' he groaned, breathless and hot. 'You need to be very, very sure.'

'We have one night, Sante,' she pleaded. 'Make it count.'

Passion flared in his eyes as he gazed into hers. 'I will.'

More than a determined acceptance of the challenge, his reply was a vow that he immediately backed up with action. He claimed her mouth again with intimate, ruthless determination, making Mia writhe and shudder in his lap. *Yes.*

They would destroy this. She moaned and restlessly stirred as he plundered her, revelling in the hard strength and fiery heat of his body and the fierce hold of his arms. She rocked against the erection digging into her side. She wanted that. She wanted all of this. Now.

He increased the pressure of his kiss and unleashed his hands to torment her more. He slipped his fingers beneath the soft tee and the track pants and skated over her skin, unerringly finding her most sensitive places.

'Sante...'

'Your skin is so soft,' he muttered. 'You're so hot.'

'Strip me,' she begged. She needed to be naked, now.

'*Soon.*'

She was rendered immobile in his hold, in this unutterable delight as he was deliciously focused on her pleasure.

'I like watching your eyes. They're beautiful,' he said, sounding awed. 'You're unbearably beautiful.'

While he was an unbearable tease. She could cry with frustration. Locked in intimacy, they kissed and kissed—the endless lush kisses sent her higher and higher into the stratosphere and his hands kept her there—hovering in a heavenly tortured sensation of want and need and desire. He groaned as he lightly stroked her slick core, and with a moan she bucked against his hand, desperately needing more—melting in the heat that burned between them. He answered, pressing more firmly, invading her in a rhythm that made her moan louder and longer—*demanding*.

'I like making you hum, Mia.' He nipped her lower lip, then licked it. 'Hum louder.' He whispered his need into her mouth. 'I want to hear you scream.'

She circled and rolled her hips as his teasing fingers became both too much and not enough.

'Sante...'

'Scream, Mia.'

He kissed her with infinite patience and overwhelming intensity. Tormented her as he stroked harder, hotter, faster. She arched, every muscle searingly tight as the sensual tension devastated her. She tore her lips free, her breath caught until with one stroke more he tipped her into a tumult of sensation that blew her mind. She screamed, utterly overwrought as pleasure rocked through her in beautiful, violent waves.

She kept her eyes closed, turning her face into his chest, trying to recover her form. But there were orgasms and then there was *that*. And she wasn't ever going to be the same.

She felt him move beneath her, gathering her in his arms to lift then gently lower her to the plush carpet. She opened her eyes in time to see him kneel beside her and whip his T-shirt off over his head.

Mia's post-orgasmic lethargy—and embarrassment— was immediately dispelled. She stared at him in awe. The candles flickered, casting warm light and secret shadow across his beautiful frame. He was *perfect*—utterly perfect. His shoulders were broad, his chest muscled, his skin smooth and tanned and she avidly watched, willing him to remove his trousers.

He didn't. He sat back and watched her, a slow smile creasing his features.

'Still hungry, Mia?'

'You know I am.' She raked her gaze down his tense frame, taking in the bunch of his muscles. 'So are you.'

His hands slid beneath the T-shirt she wore and up to cup her breasts and then he whisked the top from her body. He lowered his focus and she watched dusky colour deepen across his cheekbones.

'Indeed I am,' he murmured huskily.

He hooked his fingers into the waistband of the track- suit pants he'd loaned her and slowly tugged them down.

'You're magnificent.' He cocked his head and surveyed what he'd exposed. 'I'm going to taste every inch of you.'

She wanted that, she really did, but she wanted to see him, too. To taste him, too. But he overpowered her completely—simply with the sensations of his lips, of his hands, of the weight of his searing focus. She'd known they had chemistry. She'd been physically attracted to him from the first second she'd seen him in his office restroom. But she'd not been prepared for how intense it would be when he touched her like this. She shivered as he skimmed his palms along her arms, pressing kisses here and there—teasing in a pattern that she couldn't anticipate but that she adored as he moved closer to her more intimate parts.

'Sante...'

She didn't hide her need—indeed, she held *nothing* back. They had only one night and she wanted everything. She would absolutely indulge in her hunger for him.

'Sante...'

'One moment...' He sounded ragged as he rose away from her to pull a square package from his pocket before taking his trousers down and his briefs with them.

Mia's jaw dropped. He was *built*. And he was *hot*. For *her*.

She reached forward, barely getting the chance to trace over his perfect body before he pulled back.

'Don't...don't look at me like that,' he muttered. 'I won't last.'

'Sante...'

Expelling a pained sigh, he braced over her. Mia wriggled in delight, so ready to finally have him. But Sante, the tease, went back to savouring her. She'd not known it was possible to be so tortured and so content at the same time. His mouth was hot and his words sexy. He cupped her breasts, rubbing his thumbs over her tight nipples, rousing her until she rocked her hips towards him over and over.

'Hungry girl,' he huffed approvingly and slid lower.

He was the hungry one—lascivious in his attentions, his touches, until Mia thrashed beneath his hold and gripped his hair. She was going to come again and she wanted him with her this time.

'Sante…'

'I need you ready.'

'I am. I want you, Sante…*please*.'

He lifted his head, his breath blowing hot right where she was most sensitive. 'You want me?'

'*Now. Please.*' Breathless, she arched again and again.

He moved swiftly, abandoning the attempt to tease her more. She cupped the side of his face, feeling his flushed skin, reading the desperate tension in his body as he held her hip firm and still. Their eyes locked and he thrust hard and deep. Mia crumbled instantly, her cry high and loud as ecstasy unravelled her completely.

He growled, his teeth gritted, lodged firm and still, utterly to the hilt, as she shattered about him. As her shudders finally eased, she wrapped her legs and arms about him tightly, so entranced. It was as if eternity was unlocked in that moment. So stupid, so fanciful, but what she was experiencing was just so good. He, too, had a look of wonder on his face.

'*Oh, Sante,*' she sighed, so desperately needing more.

He broke.

'*Mia, Mia, Mia…*' He chanted her name fervently as he thrust hard and fast, utterly unleashed. But in his accent, in this moment, it was as if he were murmuring in his first language—*mine, mine, mine.*

And she was.

Mia blinked, a trickle of desolation creeping in as Sante peeled away from her body. But he immediately held his hands out to her. She automatically took them.

'Come on.' He hauled her to her feet. 'Let's get some-where more comfortable.'

He tucked her hand under his arm and picked up a couple of candles. For a moment Mia could only watch; he definitely looked like he was ready to continue. *Thank goodness.*

She watched the play of his muscles as he slowly led her up the stairs. The rain struck the windows like bul-lets. The wind howled, rattling the latches and hinges as if seeking a way to break in and tear them apart. But the wide stone of the house was too solid for the wild weather to breach. She curled her hand around his biceps, smiling at his strength. They were safe in this secret sanctuary, in the dancing, warm candlelight. She saw little of his bedroom, only the vast bed as he set the candles on the small table each side of it, illuminating the vast mattress in the middle. Mia simply crawled onto the soft sheets, ready for him.

He murmured his appreciation as she posed. 'You're an absolute goddess.'

It was such sweet, intoxicating flattery and she tum-bled into it with full enthusiasm. 'Are you going to sur-render to me?' she murmured, desperate to devastate him the way he just had her.

'Oh, no. Never.' His lips curved into a half-sorry smile. 'But I will worship you.'

And Mia never wanted the night to end.

CHAPTER SEVEN

SANTE WASN'T ABLE to do anything more than listen to the rain steadily falling and will it to continue for hours—no, days—yet, this couldn't be done. He wanted more of her. But time refused to stop and despite the heavy clouds, dawn lightened the room. The only consolation was that he could then see her properly again. Thankfully, he'd had the presence of mind to bring her to his bed. While he was used to staying up all night, she wasn't. She was deeply, beautifully asleep. For a second he pretended that last night hadn't been the best sex of his life, that it only felt like that because it had been a while. But the pathetic delusion didn't stick. It had been the best—sensational. *She* was sensational.

That first time had been too fast. He'd intended to draw her to the edge and back again to torment her for the days of sensual torture she'd put him through this week at the office. But she'd used her breathy pleas and luscious body to sever his will. So swiftly, he'd succumbed to the desire that had been killing him for days.

Now he watched, half-afraid that if he closed his eyes she might disappear. He still couldn't quite believe she'd come after him. No one did that. Not even Adele—though as he sent her a continual supply of work even when he went AWOL, Adele always knew he was alive and well.

But he'd not contacted Mia and she'd been pissed about it. She'd thought if she didn't deliver that stupid parcel he'd have fired her, but her coming here was about more than that. The way she'd *scolded* him for going silent—that he'd been rude and unfair. Ordinarily, he'd never have agreed, but he'd read and listened to her messages. She'd phoned so many times he felt bad about it. Weirdly, he also felt good. She'd persisted. She'd tried so many ways to reach him. And then she'd followed up with action. She was the only person who'd *ever* come after him.

He'd been abandoned at birth. Survived only because he had strong lungs. A foundling—unwanted, unclaimed, unknown. The first foster home had initially been okay but there was never permanence in the system. Soon, it had been another home. A bad one. Then another. Worse. He'd thought he'd secured his freedom and future in the form of a scholarship to an elite school in England…

He went rigid, refusing to think about the time he'd spent over there. The way his past intersected with Mia's would crush what was between them now. But not only had she come all this way to him yesterday, she'd also *unleashed* with him. Because she'd wanted him, and knowing that had evaporated any last resistance he could muster. Hell, his self-control had lasted less than a week and if he'd known they were going to be this fantastic together, he wouldn't have lasted an *hour* before trying to seduce her.

He slipped out of bed and went to the kitchen. Those pastries were good but they weren't enough to live on. He needed a more substantial meal and so did she. He checked the power but it was still out. Fortunately, his backup generator kept the refrigerator going and charged his phone. He scanned the trillion messages that had landed, quickly responded, making one particularly rash decision and eventually clearing the list. Then he pulled food and lit the gas. He was going for a feast—mostly to keep himself busy while she rested. He tried not to recall every moment of the night but his uncooperative brain kept sending images. She'd been so hot. So sweet. He should have stayed in bed, should have waited so he could take more from her—

'Something smells amazing.'

Sante turned. She stood in the doorway and helplessly he just took his time to look. The jut of her breasts against the soft fabric of his tee was torture. Again. And again, he was overcome by the memory of how she'd felt above, beneath, about him. He slowly drank in the sweet curves of her legs. He just wanted to sink back inside her and forget the world. But he glimpsed a mark on her thigh that hadn't been there last night. He didn't remember doing it, didn't want to hurt her in any way at all. This wasn't meant to be that intense.

'Are you hungry?' Amusement gleamed in her eyes.

Hell, he was supposed to be cooking not drooling. He spun back to the pan, quickly stirring to stop the eggs sticking. To stop his brain from spontaneously combusting at the mere sight of her.

'Very hungry,' he coughed. 'Making brunch.'

One look and he'd not just lost his words, but his capacity to think. Again.

'Can I help?' She leaned around him, wide-eyed at the number of pans.

Following her gaze, he conceded he might've gone a little overboard but he'd needed distraction. Apparently, she needed distraction, too—she nosed in the pans and would've taken the spatula off him if he didn't hold it up out of her reach.

'You don't trust me to cook?' He chuckled as her eyes widened with embarrassment.

'Clearly, you can cook.' She gestured at the overloaded cook-top. 'But I don't like doing nothing.'

Right, she was used to being the one who did things for others. It was more than her job. She cared—either as nanny, or manager—ensuring everyone had everything they needed in order to do their job.

'You could just sit down and let me spoil you.' He watched her restless discomfort with amusement. 'Or if you must move, you can find the cutlery,' he added, relenting when she clearly didn't want to remain still.

Sure enough, a relieved expression crossed her face. She set plates and cutlery in position on the table and found juice in the fridge. Sante didn't think he'd ever bothered to set the table when here alone. Food was a scoff-and-be-off thing for him. But she had it looking pretty in an instant. He poured her a coffee and she pounced on it before taking a seat and looking amused as he set the plates of food between them.

'Do you think there's enough?' she teased.

He'd not realised just how much he'd made while she slept; it had just been a way of filling in time. Mia picked up her fork and sampled the pancakes first and he froze, stupidly interested in her reaction.

'This is *really* good.' She swallowed.

'Why so surprised?' And why did he care so much?

'Sorry.' But her giggle undermined her apology. 'I didn't think you'd cook for yourself. I assumed you'd have a private chef.'

'I sent the staff home before the storm, remember?'

'But is one of them a chef?' Her eyes gleamed as he shook his head. 'There's really nothing you can't do. You're a genius at everything.'

Why did she sound annoyed about that?

'I learned to cook thanks to the internet. Utilising scraps. Actually, I worked on an app for nutrient analysis of those meals. It did well.'

'Naturally.' She watched him season the eggs. 'So you do all the cooking when you entertain here?'

Startled, he glanced up. He never had guests stay. This was his personal sanctuary; that was the point.

'Right, no entertaining.' She glanced at the window. 'Which is a shame because you could have the best summer party here.'

'You like parties?' he muttered. She'd organised a mini-party in his office for his staff.

'Sure, sometimes.' She licked her lips. 'But you prefer to be alone.'

'Sure, sometimes,' he mimicked. 'I like the space here. It's calming.'

'Your brain races.'

'Yes.' It overwhelmed him sometimes. 'I work in the garden for hours. It eases up then,' he muttered. While he did manual labour he could put all the ideas in the back of his brain to percolate.

'What about all the other properties on that list Paolo gave me?'

'Most are investments. The property team manages the leases.'

He enjoyed the acquisition process. He was careful and did diligence but ultimately it was a gut decision.

Property was tangible—literally solid, and he liked accumulating solid security. But this one was his absolute favourite. Perhaps that was because it was the nearest to the place he'd been found. Though in truth, he wasn't certain he was even Sicilian. His mother could have been from anywhere.

He watched her demolish the first pancake and saw her trying to choose between eggs and yoghurt and felt the oddest need to confess the truth—because he did *not* need to brag to her, right? 'I can only cook breakfast food. Dinner is freezer meals. Nutritious ones a private chef preps back in Rome.'

Mia paused and her eyes gleamed with surprise—and knowing pleasure. 'You should keep a store at the office so you're not starving in the morning and need pastry.'

She was right, of course. Which was annoying.

'Or I could put eggs and milk in the kitchenette and you could cook breakfast for the staff. This is impressive.' She chuckled at his expression, then glanced at the window behind him. 'The rain's pretty relentless.'

'It's forecast to ease later.' He drew breath and broached the topic that'd been bothering him since scanning his messages earlier. 'The helicopter might be able to land later, but the mayor's put a call out for help in assessing damage to the region.'

'Then surely that's the priority.'

Naturally, she would put other people before herself. His body tightened.

'It would mean you couldn't get back to Rome today,' he said. 'You'd have to spend another night here.'

She was quiet and still and looked right back at him.

He coughed. 'For the record, I'm not devastated about that idea.'

'No?'

Oh, he'd needed to see that curve in her mouth. Unable to resist a moment longer, he stalked around the table and grabbed the hem of that tormenting T-shirt with both fists. She lifted her arms, enabling him to have her naked in seconds.

'I know it's terrible to appreciate a personal win when its possibly a crisis for the others, but then, I'm a selfish jerk, right?' he said roughly, moving in close to breathe in her soft warmth. 'I already said yes to them.'

She wrapped her arms around his shoulders and her legs around his hips. 'Good.'

He groaned as she pressed her hot, wet core against him. He'd clearly been wrong about her needing a break. He hoisted her onto the table and kicked off his shorts, immeasurably glad he'd had the presence of mind to shove a condom in his pocket earlier. Her chuckle encouraged him to kiss her wilder, faster. Again.

Which meant he immediately needed another round to prove he *could* take his time.

An hour later he sprawled with her on the sofa, idly watching the rain trickle down the windowpanes, refusing to react to the intense relief streaming through his system. He didn't just have another night with her, but all of this afternoon as well. He ran his fingers through her hair, indulging in constant touch even though they were both boneless. But he would savour her silkiness, take what he could, while he could. Because it had to be enough.

'This place is just beautiful.' She gazed up at the ceiling. 'You have quite the library.'

His biggest collection was here. He could lose himself for hours in either the garden or the books.

'If I were you, I would never leave. Just work from home,' she chuckled.

'I thought I was supposed to show up more?' he teased.

She considered him, those blue eyes glinting like jewels beneath lowered lashes. 'You leave messages for them all the time in the project files.'

He tightened his arms around her, appreciating that she'd acknowledged that. But her comment about never leaving a place like this made him curious. 'You travel a lot—don't you enjoy it?'

'I can save more when the accommodation is thrown in.'

Right. He understood. He'd done the same when he'd first returned to Sicily and needed to claw his way up from nothing. But she shouldn't *need* to save money. Not only did she come from a wealthy family, her brother was also as much of a billionaire as Sante was, so why the hell had he abandoned her?

'Why do you use Simonini, not Lorenti?' he asked before thinking better of such blatant curiosity.

'It's another name from my mother's side of the family.'

'You don't want to be associated with your father?'

She turned her head and shot him a level look. 'You might have some understanding of why I wouldn't.'

He froze, regretting entering this minefield. It would kill the mood by reminding Mia of the enmity her brother had for him. This time with her now was too precious. Too short. But what of Dario? Didn't she want to be associated with him?

Sante didn't blame Mia for believing her father about the accident being his fault, that he'd accepted a pay-off.

She'd been a kid. But Dario had known Sante better than *anyone* back then. Sante had even told him a little of his childhood, yet Dario had chosen to believe the worst— that Sante had abandoned him and taken money to stay away.

Sante knew all too well that people generally believed the worst whether they knew about his past or not. He reached for his coffee, scalding his mouth instead of speaking more. Because Sante *was* selfish and he didn't want the past to ruin this moment.

'I don't believe you took money from him,' she said, eventually filling the lengthy silence that had grown.

'After a decade of thinking the worst of me?' His disbelief was immediate and impossible to contain.

Because no one had ever just believed him. Not without solid proof and even then…

Her colour deepened but her gaze remained steady. 'Yes.'

His confusion grew. 'You simply believe my word? Now? Why?'

'It's not only about believing you.' She licked her lips nervously. 'I know my father. He was a bully who did whatever he deemed necessary to get what he wanted. Including lie. He'd have thought nothing of lying about you.' She looked worried, her volume dropping. 'He told Dario you'd taken his money. He didn't want you in Dario's life.'

Sante flinched but she saw. The blooming compassion in her eyes rooted him in place.

'He had very specific plans for my brother and me, and he eliminated anything he saw as a distraction.'

Sante didn't give a damn about Dario now but he found he was curious about what Mia's father had wanted for her. Because he was fairly sure flitting from one random job to another wasn't in that snob's master plan. 'What or who did he eliminate from your life?'

Mia didn't answer. *She'd* been the distraction. *She'd* been eliminated. Not that she wasn't telling Sante that; it was irrelevant and he was only asking to avoid the crux of the conversation. He didn't trust her belief in him. But actually, this *was* exactly the sort of thing her father would have done.

'Did he chase off all the boys who flocked the second they caught sight of you?' Sante muttered.

Her father certainly hadn't liked her getting attention as she'd gotten older. But as she'd not had much from him, she'd liked it. She'd done the inevitable and made a very bad choice mostly because—despite her father's best efforts to squash her natural spirits—she'd been a romantic who believed in *love*. That full-on at-first-sight, deep and irrevocable, no-obstacle-could-ever-deny-it kind of love that only actually ever happened on a movie screen. She'd been so naive.

Mia could see Sante holding back now. In the rare instances that Dario had mentioned Sante since the accident, he'd insisted Sante was a user—only interested in people for what he could get out of them. Dario had referenced all that time he'd spent showing Sante coding and apps—which was why Mia had thought Sante had stolen Dario's idea. She knew that all Sante wanted from her was sex. But that was all she wanted from him, too, right? This was merely a wrinkle in her system that needed smoothing out. Dario would be appalled if he knew, but he never needed to. *No one* would *ever* know.

And *she* didn't need to know more about Sante. Yet,

every minute she remained here, her curiosity deepened. The fact that he was so guarded and reticent only aggravated her more. She knew little of his past other than he'd come to her brother's school on scholarship when he was in his teens. But there was nothing about him or his past online—not even anything on his company website—not that there was anything deeply unusual about that; Mia knew super-wealthy people were often notoriously private. So she didn't know where he'd gone after the accident. He'd just vanished. She'd assumed he'd returned to his home town—to his family, but he'd never mentioned any family at all and there certainly was no evidence of family here. There were no photos, no personal 'things.' The only constant person in his life seemed to be Adele. And she couldn't ask her because she was occupied caring for Bruno. She tried to remember more from the summer Sante had stayed at her father's house now. Only there was one moment she couldn't bear to touch on, and the bigger problem was Mia had been so young. The boys hadn't been around her much. Plus, they'd spoken in Italian together—the language had sounded so familiar yet was foreign to her by then. Her loss had made her ache. Her father had banned them from speaking Italian when they'd moved—they were to be English. Mia's Italian still wasn't all that great now. That was partly why she'd agreed to help Adele.

But she *wasn't* going to ask more about Sante's past. She wasn't going to pry over the boundaries they'd drawn. This wasn't anything more than a two-night stand and only about getting this chemistry out of her system. The one pure distraction was to occupy her mouth in another way entirely. This weekend *had* to fix her fascination. Her lust had to be sated because this couldn't be anything more than physical chemistry. And surely, she wasn't screwing up her job because this was only a short-term placement. This was nothing like what had happened with Oliver. She wasn't going to end up publicly shamed and fired.

When she returned to Rome tomorrow, they would move forward and forget all about it. But that meant she couldn't waste a minute on sleep now, nor on talking about things that couldn't be changed. So she turned to him, tempting him, moving with him until she simply couldn't move anymore.

Sante wasn't in bed beside her when she woke early Sunday morning. Heart seizing, Mia immediately glanced out the window. Not only had the rain stopped, the sun had actually appeared. Which meant she'd be able to leave for Rome this morning. Sucking in a breath, she swiftly grabbed her own clothes, showered and dressed. Sante was in the kitchen. He was also fully dressed, not cooking in nothing but boxers this morning. Not cooking at all. Breakfast was ready on the table but it was a cold spread and Sante was on a call. Glancing at her, he ended it and put his phone on the table.

'You must have a bunch more calls to make,' she murmured, avoiding the wariness in his eyes. 'To check on your neighbours and everyone.' She glanced at the phone. Sure enough, it was lighting up with notifications. 'I'll go for a walk in the garden while you're busy.'

He nodded. She took a bowl of fruit and yoghurt with her. She needed some fresh air and some space for herself.

The grounds hadn't suffered badly in the storm—

leaves were scattered about the place but the sodden patches were already drying out. She walked the perimeter of the small lake, drawing in the fresh air. It truly was a private paradise—those high, boring walls hid its beauty from the world. But this was definitely the place in which Sante roamed untamed—unclothed even—alone and at peace. And somehow, that thought made her heart ache. The wrought iron and glass summerhouse she glimpsed through the trees was too magical not to investigate. It was unlocked and happily also undamaged. There was some extra furniture stacked in the corner but otherwise it was carefully filled with tropical plants that had flourished through the winter. Someone took huge care of this place. Tired and struggling to keep that unwelcome sadness at bay, she sank onto the plush chaise and put her feet up. She'd had very little sleep last night and she hated the fact she still ached for more intimacy with Sante.

'Mia?'

She stirred, blinking drowsily.

'You okay?' Sante came into her view. 'You're very quiet.'

'Contrary to popular belief, I'm not a twenty-four-seven noisemaker.' She sat up, awkward and flustered.

'Okay.' He moved forward. 'So it's not that you're regretting...'

'There's nothing wrong and I have no regrets. You do more thinking than speaking sometimes. If you must know, I was napping.' She gestured around the summerhouse, wanting to move the subject on because she'd realised she'd shared too much with him this weekend.

She'd adored having sex with him but she'd liked *talking* with him as well. He was a surprisingly good listener and she'd opened herself up a little too much. She needed to rein it in. She always gave too much of herself to people who didn't actually want it. But Sante challenged the self-protective methods she'd learned to employ far too easily. Hell, he only had to look at her and her defences melted.

'The helicopter will be here in an hour. It's less than a two-hour flight to Rome so you'll be home by lunchtime.'

'Thank you. That definitely sounds better than the trip I took to get here.' She still couldn't drag her gaze from his. 'Are you coming back to Rome today?' She tensed as her stupid voice quivered.

He hesitated. 'I need to check on my neighbours in person.'

'Of course.' Mia stood.

It would be best to leave him here but she kept staring at him, and he at her, and that scorching desire rose within her again. Restless, she waved about the greenhouse. 'This place is—'

He stepped forward and *crushed* her in his arms. With a relieved moan she kissed him back—every bit as hard and as hungry. He was right. No more making polite conversation to fill in the last little time they had left together. This was her *last* chance to touch him. To explore his physical perfection. To make him quiver and shake and shout and she went for it.

'Mia,' he sighed jerkily, trying to catch her hands and wrest back control.

But she ignored him, kissing down his body and wrapping a firm hand around his shaft to hold him firm so she could tease him with her tongue and then suck him in deep and revel in his throaty groans. This was what she wanted—for him to be felled by her. And she got it—until the moment he flipped and paid her back. With interest.

Almost an hour later he pressed her to him, gently stroking her back, keeping her in place against him as they both struggled for breath. She tucked her face into the side of his neck and avoided his eyes and drew in his warmth and scent. With body and soul aching, she appreciated these last moments of intimacy. It was the sweetest embrace of her life.

Which meant it took her a moment to realise the rhythmic noise growing louder was the approaching helicopter. She startled, heart stopping.

'It's okay,' he muttered. 'It'll wait.'

No. It was time to go. The sooner she was out of here now, the better. Mia darted into the beautiful en suite and pulled herself together. Sante walked her down a winding path to a helipad. His frown was back. The square jaw. She just knew the man would say nothing so she made herself smile brightly.

'Um, thank you for...'

He just stared at her. Right. What was she thanking him for? Why feel the need to act polite as if this had been some nice social interaction, not the hottest most intense experience of her life?

She cleared her throat, determined to be resolute and dignified. 'No regrets, no repeats.'

She had to pretend as if this had never happened. As if it had just been a delicious dream.

'Back to work,' she added. 'Back to a professional distance.'

'Of course,' he muttered his agreement shortly. 'Not a problem.'

CHAPTER EIGHT

SANTE FROWNED DOWN at his pen, avoiding meeting any-one's eyes. *Especially* hers. Maintaining his professional distance was an unbearable, annoying, endless problem. He needed fewer meetings. Fewer hours in the office. Better still, none at all if he was going to survive the next two and a bit months. Three days ago he'd watched Mia board his helicopter and told himself it was the right thing.

She wanted them to be done. In truth, in that moment all *he'd* wanted to do was peel her clothes from her and make her hot and soft and his again. Which had been im-possible. And it hadn't felt right sending her back alone, either. But it was for the best.

Except it wasn't. Mia had a starring role in his dreams, night after night—fantasies, in truth, given he couldn't ac-tually sleep. He lay awake for hours, staring at the ceiling, wishing she were with him. He couldn't even concentrate on work through the night anymore. It was actually worse than last week and that had been bad enough.

It was appalling. He'd gone for *years* spending every night alone. He'd never had a relationship last more than a few weeks because his date grew impatient with his in-ability to 'open up.' Because Sante didn't share anything personal ever and he refused to *care*. Except he wanted

Mia. *All* the damned time. It was like she'd infected him somehow.

He needed distraction. *More* meetings with *more* people. That was what she'd suggested; that was what she would get. He was insanely careful not to be alone with her. He left every door open so he couldn't be tempted to touch her. Until he *had* to shut his door to try to block her dulcet tones.

He'd heard her humming this morning. She was busy, engaging as ever, clearly not suffering the same way he was. She'd sounded as if she hadn't a care in the world and he'd never felt such resentment. He'd not had a decent night's sleep since he'd first seen her. Now he'd had her, he *craved* her attention—her eyes on him, her touch. And he was jealous of an *intern*. The way she checked in with each one every morning grated. Because she didn't check in with him. She *emailed*. He emailed back. Despite being only fifteen feet away from her. His only respite should have been when she went for her customary walk at lunchtime. Instead, he spent the entire forty minutes glancing out the window, watching for her return.

He was pathetic. He was determined to regain control. But he couldn't so much as look at her while he did. Except his peripheral vision refused to play ball—it sent his brain updates of her in her long skirts and soft blouses that hinted at those glorious curves, her glossy hair in a ponytail or plait. Always stunning. Always looking like the best present a guy could ever hope to be given. But he'd never been given presents at all let alone ones to keep. That didn't stop him wanting to unwrap her, wanting to enjoy her, again and again and again.

* * *

He wouldn't so much as look at her. Didn't offer the briefest acknowledgement when she walked into the room. In fact, Sante Trovato was more grumpy than ever.

Mia was determined not to let it bother her. This was the agreement. They'd had their one night—yes, it had turned into two—but it had ended the second she boarded that helicopter. This was exactly what *she'd* wanted. So she was fine with it. Just *fine*. She wasn't going to daydream about being back in Sicily. She wasn't going to replay every second of the best sexual encounter of her life. She would move forward. *She* would be responsible and professional.

But that he could simply *blank* her? So coldly, so easily? The few times he had to speak to her, he did it without even looking at her. Which riled. Of course she'd expected him to be a little remote but really, the man was being rude.

She began counting off the days on the calendar. They'd had three days in the office since the weekend and there were still far too many to go before Adele would be back.

Her stupid body wouldn't stop aching and her brain *did* unhelpfully replay every moment from the weekend at the *worst* times during the day and rampantly at night. Which meant she tossed and turned and her exhaustion and resentment worsened by the minute. Which was frustrating given she'd been the one to stipulate they could have only that one weekend. That there be nothing more. But his cold, robotic behaviour destroyed the last of her patience. She grabbed a shirt from her wardrobe and buttoned it, pulled on a skirt. She would get through another day. She could do this.

Once in the office she glared at the terse emails and abrupt orders. There wasn't even a please or a thank-you. Absolutely no pretence at politeness. Well, she wasn't replying. He could damned well deal with her in person. But he didn't even look up when she went into his lair to inform him that the team had finished phase one of the synergy project at last.

'Make sure they test it rigorously,' he responded briefly.

'Yes, of course,' she sniped primly. 'Your wish is my command.'

She turned and glided out of his office and back to her desk. Or she would have glided if her upper arm hadn't been grasped tightly—forcing her to veer away from her destination and into the doorway five paces beyond instead.

'What the hell is that?' Sante's growl was harsh in her ear as he pulled her into the small room, pushed her against the back wall and pressed in close. His gaze skimmed down her body, his expression tightening as he saw her budded nipples poking through her blouse.

'You wore that just to torment me, didn't you?' he muttered huskily.

'What?' Mia stared, stunned by the wildness in his eyes. 'Are you ser—'

He slammed his mouth on hers.

'What are you doing?' she whispered when he broke apart but couldn't stop her hips arching forward for more contact.

'I can't sit there looking at you a second longer,' he

groaned, sliding his hand to her bottom and pulling her tightly against him. 'I can't stand it.'

'You don't look at me.'

'For good reason,' he explained bluntly, emphasising that very reason with a sharp thrust of his hips. 'In this fucking blouse—'

He kissed her again and Mia was lost. She quivered, all concern fled, all distance forgiven. There was nothing but sweet relief and *heat*. He wanted her still. He wanted her now. And *she* just wanted it all.

'What's wrong with this blouse?' she half laughed as he kissed across her jaw.

'Cream.'

She was blank for a moment before realising it was the shirt she'd worn that morning he'd arrived. With a groan she flung her arms around his neck. 'You've been so stand-offish—'

'I've been so *restrained*,' he argued, sliding his hands beneath said blouse. 'You have no idea—*how* could I look at you? Everyone would know what I want to do to you. I can't control my own thoughts.' He pressed against her with shockingly fantastic intimacy. 'Tell me it's the same for you.'

Mia tried to recover her reason but in the same instant she leaned fully against the wall, her legs trembling. 'Sante…'

'Maybe I'll just find out for myself.'

His kiss was hungry, his tongue rapacious, but it was his hands that were truly greedy. They went straight to her secret treasure and discovered *exactly* what she'd been thinking of for days now—with only a few strokes he made her shake.

'Sante.' She gasped and they both knew it for the approval it was. 'Sante,' she repeated, shuddering as he caressed her.

'You're *so* ready for me.' He looked at her with savage approval. 'I'm turned on so tight all the damned time, Mia. I just want to—'

He didn't say, he showed. Kissing her neck as his fingers teased. Excitement poured through her, heating her all the more. He stopped the stormy kisses and defiantly stared down at her as if daring her to stop him when he could feel for himself, so intimately, just how much she wanted him. How close she was to—

'*Sante.*' She struggled to catch her breath and slow them down because they were at *work*. 'This is the cleaner's closet,' she breathed, even as she rocked her hips a little, encouraging his skilful fingers to assuage that horrible ache inside.

'Yes.' He skittered and circled her slick sex in a wicked tease. 'Because someone thought it was a good idea for me to have an open-door policy and if I'm with you in there, someone could walk in at any moment.'

That was...*true*. She suddenly smiled. 'You have to admit a lot of the team has been more present in the office this week.'

'They won't get out of my face. Which is frustrating. Because do you know where I really want to put my face?'

'*Sante!*' she squeaked as he dropped to his knees before her.

He lifted her skirt and tugged her panties down just enough for him to graze her upper thighs with his lightly stubbled jaw. She slumped all her weight back against the wall and surrendered, spreading her legs and arching towards his hungry mouth.

'*Please...*' she pleaded, then moaned as he stroked her. 'Oh…'

She didn't need to beg. He was already stirring her higher with a rhythmic sweep of his tongue.

'*Oh...please!*' she sobbed, rocking against him. She ached for the release that was suddenly so close.

But as her arousal soared, she gasped, eyes widening as she neared the pinnacle. But it gave her the briefest glimpse of their surroundings. Of *reality.*

'I can't.' She clutched his shoulders even as she rocked against him, simultaneously panicked and shuddering and turned on even more. 'I'll be too loud.'

'I like you best when you're loud,' he said deeply.

Desperately, with her last functioning brain cell she rationalised—the others were in the meeting room so surely they wouldn't hear her from here? And with another stroke of his tongue she was too far gone to care.

'Be loud. Come on, Mia. Let me taste you. Let me hear you again.'

Oh, my. She almost crumpled as he double fingered her and fastened his hot mouth to suck her off strong. She bucked but he just worked harder, lashing his tongue over her. Oh, she wanted him. This. Now. *Always.* They were both starving and now unleashed, there was no stopping either of them. His stubble burned like an intimate fire against her sensitive skin, stirring her higher. She was so completely his.

'You're so hot, so fast for me,' he muttered. 'Come on me, Mia.'

His commanding growl unleashed her entirely. She

tunnelled her fingers through his hair, holding on in sheer joy as he devoured her, pulling her over the precipice into velvety decadence. So quickly. She closed her eyes, convulsing as waves of pleasure washed through her.

'Oh, Sante.' She gasped and pressed her palm to her mouth to muffle the sobbing scream as her orgasm rocked her.

When she finally opened her eyes she saw triumph and demand glowing in his. But he shook his head as he rose and he drew her hand away from her mouth.

'You should never silence yourself,' he muttered roughly.

That was nice and all but there was reality to face. 'We're at *work*.' She shivered.

This had been a mistake. A gorgeous, desperate, but definite mistake. Work and home and life might be one and the same for him but it wasn't for her. There were people out there. People who could have walked in on them at any moment. Who could have heard. People whom she wanted to respect her—not talk and whisper behind her back. She bent her head. This was lust. Nothing but lust. And she couldn't let herself be carried away by it.

Leaning close, he tilted her chin, forcing her to meet his fiery, intent expression. 'We're not done,' he breathed. 'You *know* we're not done.'

As she could feel his hard erection pressing against her bare thigh, she'd pretty much grasped that fact, yeah. And her own arousal was building shockingly quickly again.

'Not *here*,' she whispered fiercely while she could still think. 'I'll sleep with you again, but *not* at work.' She couldn't stop herself capitulating, but she needed this bargain. 'This can't encroach here at all. Not again.'

He drew in a breath. 'Then come to my apartment to-night.'

She shook her head. She couldn't be seen with him. 'Discreetly, Sante.'

'We're the last to leave work anyway. No one will see us. We can order in.'

So he assumed they'd dine together again as well?

Mia avoided his eyes by straightening her clothing, trying to haul together her scattered wits and regain some control over this. The fact was animal instinct had already won.

'Okay.'

She was doing a good job here and she could keep that as a separate thing. The fire between her and Sante was far more difficult to manage. So she wouldn't spend the entire night with him. She would have what she wanted and then return to her own place. The reality was this affair wouldn't last the duration of her contract. Sante was fast moving and would likely get bored—so she needed to take what she could, while she could. And as she was leaving in a few weeks, the lapse in professional judgement wouldn't matter. This was a private thing between her and Sante—one they needed to burn through. Because it was one she simply couldn't deny. But she was determined to do an even better job of managing the office. She would have nothing said against her work ethic. Ever. And as she now felt the best she had since the weekend, she could actually focus. She sat at her desk and pulled out the raft of notes she'd made from Adele's day.

'You realise it's an hour since everyone else left?'

Mia jumped, spinning her chair slightly, startled to see Sante standing just behind her.

'What's so absorbing?' His attention had flicked to her screen. 'A new software?'

'I'm updating the onboarding manual with some of the notes Adele gave me. As she knows everything about this place, I figured it would be helpful if everyone could access her usual processes.'

'You mean you've devised a way to stop the coders asking you stupid questions all the time.'

She smiled slightly. 'It's just an online reference as backup.'

He reached across and flicked through a couple of the files she'd created. 'It's simple, easy to use, pertinent information. You're really good at this.'

'Is that so surprising?' Mia asked.

But his attention had dipped to her blouse. He lifted a finger, pushing to release the top button of her vee, taking her from perfectly appropriate to provocative.

'Sante?' she whispered.

'Mmm?'

'Do you think because I've got boobs I can't have brains as well?' she murmured. 'As if it's possible to have only one or the other?'

His gaze shot back to her face and he flushed. 'Of course not.'

Mia giggled.

Sante gaped for a split second, then laughed. '*I'm* the one with no brain. I apologise. I got distracted.'

'Maybe try keeping your eyes *up*.'

'It's very difficult.'

'We're in a work setting.'

'*Empty* work setting. And it's still difficult.' He watched as she closed down the computer systems. 'Why didn't you go to university? Surely, your family has been going to Oxford or Cambridge for years?'

Mia stiffened, surprised he'd asked her something personal.

He chuckled. 'Relax, I'm not some higher education snob. You know I don't even *have* a degree.'

She didn't know that actually. She knew very little about his past other than that he'd been on scholarship to her brother's school for a couple of years.

'Didn't you go to some elite boarding school like Dario—surely that would have set you up?'

She swivelled in her seat, looking up as he leaned against her desk. He had his sleeves rolled up and his expression was relaxed and open. The most tempting man she'd ever seen in her life. Desperate to stop herself launching into his arms again here at *work*, she answered. There was no better way of cooling her jets than by thinking of her father.

'My father certainly felt I should've been more grateful for that investment, but boarding school wasn't for my benefit. It was for his. I didn't fit in. Sang too loud to make the choir. Laughed too much to be studious enough for the advanced class…but he didn't want me at home much. I spent almost every holiday being taken on school trips that I was "lucky" to go on.'

Admittedly, the extracurricular excursions had given her a bit of a travel bug.

'You were home the summer that I visited,' he said.

'Because he was away for most of it.' She watched him. 'I didn't like you,' she admitted huskily. But she'd been *fascinated* by him.

'No?' His eyebrows arched. 'I wasn't the right kind to fit in?'

'No, it wasn't that. You guys didn't even notice me,' she elaborated slightly. 'You were so busy with all your plans and I was alone.'

His gaze narrowed and his mouth opened and suddenly she didn't want to talk about what had happened towards the end of that summer. The day her father had come home unexpectedly and trampled her heart. She'd been a stupid, lonely kid who'd once again acted on a foolish impulse. But hopefully, Sante didn't remember because he had been so busy with Dario.

'Of course he wanted me to go to university.' She redirected the conversation just in case. 'He also wanted to dictate where I went and what I studied. He threatened to disinherit me if I didn't go, while at the same time moaned about having to make a donation to the university to wield enough influence to ensure my acceptance. I told him to cut me off.'

'Did he?'

She shot him a look. 'You know he was transactional. Do what he wants and he'll pay. But if you don't, then he'll withhold.'

'Not just money, affection and attention, too?' Sante said.

Yes. '*Everything* with him was conditional. And when I couldn't do what he wanted, didn't dress the way he wanted, I wasn't the right size, I didn't speak properly, and when I did I was too loud. The pathetic thing is even when I tried to do as he wanted, I could never get it right. I could never fit the mould he wanted. I tried so hard, but I'd only last a few days and revert to type—I'd laugh too loud, take another biscuit, sing too much. I'd been free at my mother's, maybe a little wild. But Westwick was so cold and I don't mean the weather. If I partially succeeded, he'd become more strict, constantly shifting the boundaries so I would always fail. Eventually, I realised I was *never* going to be what or who he wanted. He said it himself. I was too much like my mother. He'd never wanted me and he didn't like me. *I* was the distraction so I was eliminated. And in the end I rebelled— deliberately became "more." Too much. When I was seventeen I took myself right off the rails just to provoke him into pushing me away completely.'

Mia stopped, stunned that she'd just unloaded all that onto Sante of all people. It took less than two seconds for embarrassment to smother her.

'See?' she tried to joke. 'Too much. Like that. Always.'

He was clearly stunned, too. Silent and frowning. Sante slowly drew breath but she prattled on before he could offer any awkward platitude.

'Anyway, I'm starving,' she lied. 'Shall we go?'

He simply nodded.

Sante's car was powerful and utterly comfortable, but not flashy, which made her smile. Music played the second he started the engine but he flicked it off.

'Leave it on if you want. I love that song,' she murmured.

It would help cover the cringy silence enveloping them.

'Yeah,' Sante muttered.

She glanced at him as he put it back on. His cheeks were slightly flushed but he said nothing more. She'd discovered his apartment was only twenty minutes from the office when she'd tried to track him down last Friday, and again she wondered why he crashed at work as often as he did given it was so close. She bit the inside of her lip so as not to ask. Not that nor the other billion questions flooding her mind.

Like the palazzo in Sicily, his apartment block was outwardly imposing with an impenetrable brick facade. But once inside, Mia was hit with colour and comfort. The place was larger than it appeared from the outside and filled with bright furnishings and lush plants, and shelves straining beneath the weight of books with no curated orderly sense. They were piled haphazardly with no discernible cataloguing system whatsoever. Mia grinned, certain he'd be able to find whichever tome he wanted regardless. She was absurdly pleased that he had a sanctuary space here, too. She studied the series of photographs forming a massive feature wall. They were landscape shots. She recognised one taken in the grounds of the palazzo. He clearly loved that place. But the others—an ocean view through an archway, a mist-filled forest, a waterfall— they were all beautiful.

'No family photos?' she murmured.

There'd been none at the palazzo, either—only those beautiful frescoes on the walls. She kept a gallery on her phone but she always travelled with a framed picture of her mother.

'No.'

His finite response was typical closed-book Sante, but she'd offloaded earlier because he'd asked a personal question; maybe she would reciprocate and balance the scales the tiniest bit.

'None of you, either.' She faced him. 'You don't like having your photo taken?'

Sante just stared back at her. His silence was both pointed and prickly. But as he remained there—still and silent—she saw heat build in his eyes.

Right. So much for balancing the scales. They were only about a *physical* affair and she needed to reel in any other interest in him.

'Not going to send me any nudes then, huh,' she noted, covering her frustration with a little tease. 'You realise that means you don't get any from me, either.'

His stunned expression made her yelp with laughter.

'Don't want any,' he declared, stepping forward and pulling her into his arms. 'I'll settle for nothing less than holding the real thing.'

CHAPTER NINE

SANTE PRESSED HER CLOSE, sharp satisfaction rippling through him from having her in his arms again. He'd hated what she'd told him about her childhood. He remembered her as a scamp of a girl. Loud, yes. Full of laughter. Forever singing. Until her jerk of a father had come home. Lord Westwick had briefly called in twice that summer. Dario had turned resentful and silent each time his father had appeared, but it was the second visit that had particularly hurt Mia. Sante hoped she'd forgotten but she likely hadn't and he wasn't about to remind her. He knew better than anyone that there was no fixing the past.

So he kissed her, knowing he could make her feel good in that one way at least, barely restraining the urge to haul her straight to his bedroom. *Patience.* The food he'd ordered was about to arrive and she'd said she was hungry, so he forced himself to relax and release her.

'Another enormous sofa!' Mia laughingly gestured towards it with a flourish. 'I know you work almost all of the time, but when you drag yourself away you really know how to relax.'

'You think I should live in some kind of medieval

prison—all hard stone and discomfort?' he asked dryly. 'Is that what I deserve?'

She shot him an arch look. 'What do you think you deserve?'

He smiled. He liked her coy and playful. This way they could avoid untangling the knot of personal information she'd offloaded in the office. She obviously didn't want to talk about it more. Her father was an absolute jerk. So was her brother. End of story. He and she were here now only for physical release together. No feelings. No sharing of anything more than their bodies and enjoyment of food and superficial things. That was all this was.

'Clearly, I think I deserve to lose myself in soft, warm things at the end of the day...' He walked back to her.

The sharpness in her eyes heated and he abandoned any idea of patience—

The doorbell rang. Expelling a rueful sigh he whirled away to fetch the food. He forced himself to slow down— actually put the succulent lamb on plates for them to savour.

'I don't get to try the freezer meals?' she chuckled.

'They're just fuel. This is more of a feast.'

Her smile widened. 'Sounds wonderful. What did you order?'

'It's a surprise.' He was oddly nervous about pleasing her.

She set the table—fossicking in his kitchen without asking. He was absurdly happy to let her. After all, dining with her was a tormenting sensual pleasure of its own and he liked taking the time to appreciate it with her. She was as much of an enthusiast as he—just a little more audible, and her appreciation of the creamy sauce only added to his building desire.

'Oh, that's goooood,' she moaned as she tasted the sharp bite of the blue cheese sauce.

He smiled. '*Sì.*'

She eventually sat back with a resplendent sigh. 'I *was* really hungry.'

'I still am,' he muttered bluntly, rising to pull her out of the chair.

He was an absolute hedonist when it came to Mia. She unleashed every appetite he had and better still, she met his with her own. He ignored the plates and mess. It was his turn to explore. Her curves. Her heat. Hands-on and hungry, he wanted her in his bed *now*.

'Rules,' he said huskily while he could still remember that he still needed boundaries.

'Rules?' She blinked. 'What—'

'You're only sleeping with me for the foreseeable future.'

Not that there was a future. This was not forever. This was only now.

'Ditto, obviously,' she said haughtily. 'And it ends when my contract ends.'

'Obviously,' he echoed her bite.

'And *nothing* more at work.'

What did that matter when she was leaving in only weeks? Every scruple about being her boss was long burned by lust, but he agreed anyway. 'If I know you're going to be in my bed every night that'll make that easier.'

'Every night?' Her eyes widened. 'Then you won't be pulling all-nighters at work anymore.'

'You work from home with me on Fridays.'

'Home?'

'Sicily.'

She frowned. 'You mean I do a four-day week because let's get real, I won't be working.'

'You work long hours already. Consider it time in lieu.'

Enough negotiation. There was only one thing he could do now because there was nothing he liked more than making her limp and speechless, pink cheeked and panting with that stunned-but-sated dreaminess in her big blue eyes.

He worked her hard, savouring her warmth and strength until at last she lay sleepy and quiet, snuggling close. Her beautiful smile pulled his own from him. *Sì*, rendering this beautiful bundle of positive effervescence into a speechless heap of lax limbs was about the most rewarding thing he'd ever set his mind to.

She sprawled over him like a soft blanket. 'You really like a landscape.'

Sante fiercely protected both his privacy and autonomy. He never wanted to factor anyone else in his decisions. He was selfish. But being free to make his own decisions, not to be constrained or have judgement poured over him, was as essential to him as breathing. Yet, Mia's genuine appreciation, the fearless interest in her eyes, touched him.

'The one on the far left is the view from my property in the South of France.'

'Ooh la la.'

He chuckled. 'They're views from all my various properties.' He liked having the gallery here to remind him of what he'd achieved when he was working hard. And that he had places to go should he need to. Always.

Mia lifted her head and studied the frames. 'Is there more than one view from each, or one from each property?'

'You think there's too many? That I'm greedy?'

'No. When you've known deprivation or uncertainty, then you need as many as you can hang on to.'

'Deprivation?' He stiffened. Had Dario told her about his childhood?

'Are you saying you had everything you ever wanted in your childhood, Sante?'

'No one does,' he deflected with a generalisation. 'You didn't.'

That silenced her. For a moment.

'So it's pictures of places not people.'

He combed through her hair gently. Curious thing she was. No people because he had no family. He had no pictures of himself even—why would he ever want to dwell on his past?

'There's more permanence with places.' He opted to keep it light. 'Most of them are investments.'

'Investments. So you don't invest in people?' She shook her head. 'Your tech incubator is important to you,' she added. 'You want them to feel comfortable.'

'So they make me more millions. Isn't that what you said?' he murmured.

She turned to look down into his eyes. 'I think underneath the isolationist exterior you're still a team player.'

'That was the only way to get ahead back then. I had to play the game until I was wealthy enough not to have to bother.'

'So because you're ludicrously wealthy now you think the rules no longer apply to you?'

'I don't go around just doing anything I want at any time.'

'No?' She actually giggled.

'No. I'm being incredibly restrained right now.'

Her eyebrows arched. He rolled, pinning her with his body. Yet, instead of distracting her, his own curiosity was engaged.

'Don't you want a home of your own?' Why didn't she have cosy sofas with blankets and books when she clearly appreciated them? She should be the vibrant chatelaine of some vast manor, all cashmere sweaters and surrounded by adoring dogs. 'What happened to Westwick?'

Presumably, her father's estate in Wiltshire was now Dario's.

Mia stiffened beneath him. 'I don't want to be tied to one place.'

He didn't believe her. But he understood why she wouldn't have fond memories of that place.

'Everyone wants their own space they can feel safe in.' To have things that brought comfort or peace. For him that was space, greenery, solitude—a *view.* But Mia had too much heart to settle for that. She would need company of the canine kind at least. He inhaled, about to ask her—

'That's usually just my bedroom. Speaking of, it's late. I should get home.' She wriggled, trying to get out from under him.

'The agreement was every night.'

'But not *all* night,' she said. 'We only have that in the weekend.'

Huh. Sante never normally acknowledged weekends. Every day was the same. Sleep. Wake. Work out. Work. Eat. Sleep. In whichever of his abodes he felt like at the time. But now he *lived* for the weekend. For having day time with her again that wasn't constrained by workplace etiquette or a finite few hours in the evening.

The first Friday through Sunday was a pure romp— sex followed by food followed by a teasing debate about music, and then she'd tried to trounce him on the gaming console he'd brought with him. It was fantastic. But still not enough.

Despite knowing she would be in his bed every evening, the days at work became an annoyance. The brief moments he was unable to touch her caused a slow rising sense of panic in him. But then she was beside him again and he relaxed.

They quickly fell into a routine. He discovered that he could cope better at work if he spent more time in the open-plan area—so he could see her, not just hear her. But by the last half hour he was so hopelessly distracted, he had to seek space in his office again so he could choose which restaurant to order from, while she made 'end of day conversation' with his recruits as they left. He knew this fascination would pass, but he was ridiculously glad she was contracted for a couple months yet.

'Sante?'

He glanced up and saw Mia standing five paces into his office, wide-eyed and waiting for him to answer some question he'd not even heard. He just gazed at her, absurdly pleased to see her even though it had only been minutes.

'Did you hear me?' Paolo said.

Sante blinked. He'd not only failed to hear his lawyer, he'd not even *seen* him, either.

'Sorry.' He frowned, swiftly dealing with Paolo's query.

Mia lingered in his office until the lawyer left.

'What were you thinking?' she muttered the second the main door banged shut.

'How much I want you.' The embarrassing thing was that was *all* he was thinking almost all the time.

'Well, stop.'

'You think I haven't tried?'

'Not hard enough.'

He walked around his desk. 'Let's understand what's hard, shall we?'

'Sante…' Shaking her head she backed away.

But she was smiling and he wanted to make her hum.

'Surely, everyone has left now,' he muttered. 'Come on, let's go.'

He drove her home. She set the table—it was a little ritual now. Twenty minutes later dinner arrived. They were working through the best restaurants in Rome but Sante was increasingly tempted to *take* her to one—he wanted to sit opposite her, take time over five or so courses—not being able to touch her as intimately as he wanted would be a delightful torture, seeing her savour the fine food another pleasure. *Sì*, he was a masochist.

Hours later she stirred. 'It's late.'

'It is.' Right now he didn't think he could move. Didn't want to. And he really didn't like her leaving his bed in the middle of the night.

'I don't have your stamina. I can't stay awake all night. The shifts on the boat are too long as it is.'

It was good she'd not had to work twenty-four or more; it wasn't healthy. He'd done it out of necessity—coding his first app through the night, working on the docks during the day. It had become habit. In truth, working all hours had been a salve. It helped him avoid the midnight demons that haunted him. Because he remembered nights in his life when he'd been utterly alone and unbearably afraid. He closed his mind to those memories and focused on Mia. She was a far better salve than work. He kissed her gently, slowly building her up until she shuddered in his arms and sighed—wanting to make her sleepy and lax and *unable* to move. But when he pulled her close after her release, he felt her summon resistance with a deep breath.

'I *really* better go,' she sighed.

'I don't want you to.' He felt a lurch in his chest as he muttered it. He wanted to walk it back right away. But it didn't matter; she was shaking her head.

'You'll be sick of me sooner if we don't have some time separately.'

'What?'

She laughed. 'I'm a lot. You know I can be a lot.'

'A lot in a good way.'

She rolled her eyes. 'Trust me, you'll have had enough, soon enough.'

He remembered what she'd said about not fitting her father's mould. 'You don't seriously think people get sick of you?'

'My mother, father and brother all did at various points and it's been a continuing theme. Which is truly pitiful, so it's really better if I—'

'You know you're perfect,' he muttered.

'*No one* is perfect, Sante. Especially not me.' She slid out of his bed and pulled on her top. 'You don't need to flatter me. I'm just tired.'

Then she should stop getting dressed and just lie down

with him again. He frowned. 'I know your father was a jerk, but your mother? I thought—'

'I loved her,' Mia interrupted, instantly defensive and fully regretting her casual admission of what was actually a deeply vulnerable truth. 'Absolutely loved her.'

And she'd loved this last week with Sante, too. But she didn't want to stay the night. She didn't want anything in their arrangement to change because she didn't want it to end too soon. She avoided his frowning gaze and talked. Her mother was a good diversion while she dressed.

'She was full of vitality,' she rambled. 'Lovely to everyone and everyone loved her. Vivacious and larger than life with a laugh that was infectious—'

'She sounds like you.'

Mia smiled sadly. That wasn't quite the compliment he'd maybe meant it to be. 'I'm the spitting image of her. Not good in my father's view. He took one look at me and the lectures began. *Don't eat so much, you don't want to get fat like your mother.*'

Sante's jaw dropped. 'Mia, you're—'

'I know, it's okay.' She smiled.

She'd worked hard to overcome the shame and guilt instilled by her father. The belief that she was too greedy, too big. He'd constantly berated her for not being slim— that she wouldn't make a desirable match if she was overweight. Because a desirable match was all she was good for. Yet ironically, the bigger she'd grown—at least those particular parts of her, the breasts, the hips, the butt—the more desirable she'd seemingly become. But that attention hadn't been the 'desirable match' kind. It had been lascivious and basic.

Yes, this affair with Sante was purely a physical thing

but she revelled in his appreciation of her—it was different. Where other men had expressed attraction it was often by leering, voicing unwanted requests for photos and crude comments—seeing her only as a body. And aside from Oliver she'd kept every one of them at a distance. But Sante savoured her in a way that was so tender it was utterly shattering. Aside from the time he'd totally lost control in the office store cupboard, he was slow and careful and such a tease. And while that cupboard moment never should have happened, it was the hottest experience of her life, and again he'd been all about pleasing *her*.

'Apparently, I took up too much space and I made too much noise.' Mia cleared her throat. 'He said my mother was an addict—to food. Alcohol. Drugs. Sex. And that I was going to be the same what with my addictive personality. I needed to tone down. I was too loud, too raucous, too curvy, to be taken seriously. *Don't overindulge like your mother. Don't be a slut like your mother.*' She paused. Then conceded. 'I mean, my mother *did* like a party. She would host all the time at our place in Capri. It was beautiful and sunny and possibly hedonistic.' She remembered the house being full of people—of *men*. Lots of laughter and doors closing on more laughter. 'Looking back I realise now she was masking unhappiness. But she needed her time out from me, too. She would get Dario to take me away to the gardens.'

She'd probably had headaches, jaded from partying all night. But as a little girl, Mia had only seen the sparkling gowns and smiles and she'd wanted to stay. It had hurt to be denied.

'And then she overdosed.'

Right. He knew. Dario would have told him.

'You moved to England.'

'To cold rules and impossible expectations and boarding school.' She nodded. 'I got in trouble at school, too. So then to another more strict one. Basically boot camp. And I was still too loud. I've been told to be quiet or go away too many times in my life to count.

'He tried to starve the love of life out of me but I can't compress myself into something I'm not.' She sighed. 'The irony was I *did* listen to some of his rubbish. I kept my virginity for years until…'

She trailed off. She'd not wanted to have her worth determined by her ability to secure a man. She'd not wanted to be 'too much' and rejected again.

Sante's eyes widened comically. 'Until?'

She sat on the edge of the bed. 'I was a naive fool. You have my permission to laugh.'

'Why? What happened?'

'As soon as I left school I got a job as a nanny. I figured it was a good match—use my "too much" energy to entertain small children. Plus, it was live-in, which meant I could leave home. There were loads of staff—maids, gardeners, drivers, secretary—the works. Two children. The parents were nice. The father had a brother who would visit sometimes.'

'And he wanted you,' Sante guessed.

'He pursued. It was very flattering. I liked the attention. I thought it was true love. As I said, I was very naive.'

'Because it wasn't true love?'

Mia bit her lip. 'I fell *hard*. I wasn't discreet—blurring boundaries between my work and personal life. I was unprofessional and distracted and young. All the staff knew we were sleeping together. What I didn't know was that all of them also knew he had a girlfriend. And all of them watched while I found that out in a public setting when he brought her to a family dinner and I had to sit there and take instruction and—'

It had been the most humiliating, shameful moment of her life. Worse than anything before. But she saw the anger in Sante's eyes and spoke before he could. 'I was a fool, Sante. It was my fault.'

'How? For thinking he cared for you?' Sante looked tense. 'He *lied* to you. And your colleagues were awful for setting you up. They were *bullies*.'

She'd thought so. But she'd also realised that she wasn't someone anyone wanted forever. Her father had said she was just like her mother—'fun for now,' not forever. Her father certainly hadn't wanted her. And sure enough, Oliver had only wanted her for *fun*. She was a good-time girl who actually hadn't had that many good times and who'd been more naive than people would have believed. Because she'd also realised that it was her pride that was hurt more than her heart.

'I fell for the *attention* he gave me,' she said. 'For the fairy tale he spun. I thought I'd found a family I could fit into. Instead, I wrecked a job I'd actually enjoyed before getting so giddy I failed to perform. I can't let that happen again.'

But now she'd had a taste of true sensual passion, she wanted more. Her father had always berated her appetite. She was voracious, wanting more than was proper or *allowed*. She didn't want anyone putting limits on what she could or couldn't have. Maybe she would take what she wanted. Claim it for herself. She shouldn't have listened to her father—shouldn't have equated lust with shame or her value with her virginity. That appetite—*any* appetite—was a bad thing. She should have let herself indulge in all pleasures *including* sex. Because it was so very good. And maybe if she'd had more, she wouldn't be making more of *this* now with Sante than what there actually was.

'Now you never stay long in the one place,' Sante murmured.

It was better not to stick around anywhere for too long. But there were other reasons for her choices. 'Travel enriches my life. I like meeting new passengers and crew. I like the variety.'

'You could still travel *and* have a home for yourself, so you're not living out of a few bags.'

'I like a nomadic existence.'

'No. You're saving for a *reason*.' He leaned up on his elbow and looked into her eyes. 'You should be living on some vast country estate with a bunch of dogs around you.'

Mia froze, *horrified*.

'I remember,' he whispered. 'You brought that stray puppy home that summer the day your dad came home unexpectedly.'

She'd really hoped Sante *hadn't* remembered that—hoped he'd been too busy with Dario to have paid much attention to an episode that had been utter heartbreak for her. But this was Sante and he had a brain bigger than Jupiter. 'I don't want to talk about that.'

She walked to the door but in seconds felt Sante gently take her arms from behind and pull her back against his warm body. 'You loved it.'

She'd wanted to.

Mia bent her head. She'd been such a fool. She'd wanted a friend. She'd wanted something to love. Something to love her back, too. That puppy had been *so* precious and she'd thought it could be hers. It had come from the farm down the road. She'd convinced the farmer's wife that her father would let her have one. The woman had always been kind to her. But Mia had lied—she'd been naive and impulsive and she'd thought she could keep it hidden somehow. But her father had arrived home unexpectedly that very night.

'*That half-breed mutt isn't staying in my house*,' Sante quoted her father, sympathy roughening his voice. 'For a moment I'd thought he'd meant me.'

Mia closed her eyes, horrified.

'He was so mean to you,' he muttered, turning her in his arms and carefully pulling her closer still. 'I heard you crying half the night.'

'You know me, never quiet.' She swallowed, tried to smile. Failed. 'Dario came and checked on me.'

'We should have done better for you that day.' Sante pressed her against his chest. 'I'm so sorry, Mia.'

'There was nothing either of you could have done. Nothing would have changed his mind. He only ever wanted his posh tweeds and pure breeds. Hunting dogs in the kennels not the house and he never wanted…'

Her, either. And definitely not some cute mutt that she'd loved instantly and unconditionally. But her father had taken that puppy and she'd never seen it again. It had just *disappeared*.

'Mia.' Sante stroked her back so tenderly. 'You should

have everything you want now. You should have a big home filled with dogs.'

No. Losing her puppy had hurt too much. She wasn't doing that again.

'You shouldn't be taking jobs with accommodation included so you can save more. You should have inherited far *more* than enough to buy yourself a home in a place you love,' he said harshly. 'What happened? *Why* didn't you get your birthright?'

She straightened and looked into his face, reading his frustration. 'It's not that straightforward, Sante.'

Her father spared a little more time for Dario but that was because he was the son and heir. Her father hadn't just disinherited Mia. He'd made those threats to her brother, too.

'Isn't it? Dario inherited the world and made his own fortune, yet he's left you with nothing. *How* is that possible?' Outrage burned in Sante's eyes.

In this past week they'd not mentioned her brother by tacit agreement. Apparently, now there was no avoiding it.

'I didn't *want* anything from my father and I didn't want Dario's help.'

'Not good enough. He should have insisted. If I had a sister there's no way I'd let her have nothing while I got everything.'

'If you had a sister you would know how difficult it would actually be, because she'd be even more boneheaded than you,' Mia fired back. 'The fact is Dario had strings as well.'

Her brother didn't trust her entirely, either. And as she was fooling around with the man he hated, maybe he'd been right to doubt her.

The ire in Sante's expression simply grew.

'He *cares* about me.' She tempered her tone and shrugged. She didn't have many memories of her life before her mother's death but she remembered a couple of times when Dario had kept her distracted. 'He protected me when we were young.'

'Not just your father. You mean in Italy.'

She nodded. She hadn't understood the extent to which Dario had protected her and that it was hard for him to let that habit go. 'We were young when she died. In England we were separated for school and most holidays so we didn't spend much time together. And then...'

'The accident.'

'His recovery took a long time,' she said softly. 'He became distant.'

Mia had been kept away from Dario—she was 'too loud'; she would impede his convalescence. So she'd felt she was little more than an annoyance to her brother as well.

'So with all that happened, we're not as close as you might think.' Not as close as she would like. 'He's used to making all the decisions and when my decisions aren't the ones he'd make, then he struggles. I would have burned anything he gave me and he knows that.'

Sante frowned. 'Mia...'

'*No one* will control me,' she said. 'And I don't need rescuing. I can manage perfectly well on my own.'

'You shouldn't have to—'

'I don't need *billions*. I don't need to acquire an infinite number of properties to feel secure. I just need to feel free to be myself.'

His lips twitched. 'For the record, accumulating an

infinite number of properties is a hugely satisfying endeavour.'

'Money and power aren't what really matter. *People* are.' Mia gazed into Sante's suddenly stiff face.

Looking at his physical perfection, no one would believe he'd ever been in an accident where the car was completely smashed. There wasn't a visible mark on him but there were scars on the inside, and her brother would always be a shadow between them. But she braced. 'I know you didn't want to leave him in the car. I know you tried everything you could to help him...'

He froze. Then moved. Stepping back and releasing her. 'You wanted to get home.'

She stepped forward. 'I *know*, Sante.'

'A week ago you thought I was a monster.'

'I saw your feet,' she said, bullishly not moving a muscle so he couldn't get past her. 'I didn't connect the dots until recently. Your shoes were worn. Your socks were bloody. You'd run for *hours*.'

'Run *away*, according to your father.'

'You *never* would have done that. I think you ran to try to get help.'

He stood, completely silent. Mia watched the shadows deepen in his eyes. Had she taken this too far? She was good at that but she wasn't going to apologise for it this time. Sante had such a *closed* life.

His lips twisted. 'I went in the wrong direction. I was disoriented. I didn't know where I was—'

Sante broke off. He'd not intended to discuss this with her again. Before her he'd not discussed it with anyone since the relentless interrogation in the police car when he'd been picked up. He'd run through the night. In the dark, cold, terrified. Devastated at leaving Dario. He'd hated that he'd had to leave him. He'd never wanted to leave someone he considered a brother. Not *again*.

'You were in shock. You'd probably had a knock to the head. Did anyone even check you out?'

'I was fine,' he muttered dismissively.

'No, you weren't.' She moved forward, planting herself right in front of him, her eyes wide and beseeching and beautiful. 'You ran for hours trying to get help for your injured friend.'

He couldn't hold that gaze. Couldn't stop the whisper from escaping. 'I thought he was going to die. I couldn't get him free. I didn't want to leave him.'

'You've never told him any of that?'

'I couldn't get to see him.'

'Dario didn't regain consciousness until two days later,' Mia explained quietly. 'He was in a bad way for a long time. Alone a long time struggling with it. My father told him you'd taken his pay-off. That you'd bargained the amount upwards to go quickly and quietly.'

'You're able to believe that your father would lie about it. But Dario still believes I would do something that awful. He never tried to find out my side of the story. He just accepted it as fact.'

Dario was like his father—entitled and ruthless. Able to just cut someone out of his life, no matter how they'd been treated. No matter that Sante had trusted Dario more than anyone in his life at that time. Dario had done it to Mia, too, hadn't he? By not supporting her.

'*You've* never talked to him about it, either. You're *equally* stubborn,' Mia pointed out. 'Maybe you should tell him the truth.'

'It wouldn't matter what I said.' Sante shook his head. 'It's easier to believe the worst of someone than the best,' he said. 'Everyone always does that.'

Mia looked at him sadly and he braced. He didn't want to hear whatever she thought she could say to make this better. There was no making it better and he didn't want to revisit this ever again. He didn't want to see compassion in her eyes. He didn't deserve it. He hadn't abandoned Dario, but he wasn't worthy of her belief in him being a decent person. Because he'd failed before.

He stood, frozen. Driving her home felt impossible. He could summon a driver, but that was an admin step too far. And now he needed to silence not just her, but the memories swirling in his head. There was only way to blank out the world. The best way. He pulled her close and to his immense pleasure, she melted.

CHAPTER TEN

SANTE SPENT THE last hour of the workday gaming with a couple of the younger coders, desperately filling in the time before he could touch her again. He'd not gamed in so long—he'd stopped when he'd left the UK and had just worked all the time. He'd forgotten it was fun—though in this moment it was basic distraction and barely working. Work was impossible—he couldn't stop dwelling on what Mia had said last night. He was furious with her family for crushing her spirit and making her feel flawed. She wasn't. She really—

'Did you learn to code at school, Sante?'

Sante glanced at Roberto, momentarily stunned. He would talk product, programming or problems, but the personal was irrelevant and every other employee knew it.

'Was it at school or did you pick it up yourself?' Roberto added. 'I mean, did it just come easily?'

'Sorry to interrupt.' Mia appeared behind them so quickly she had to have been hovering. 'Roberto, I need you and Davide to fill in this sheet for me before you go, okay?'

Sante avoided Mia's eyes, knowing she wasn't sorry at all. Both techs immediately followed her before Sante had the chance to drum up a vague but finite response for the guy. He stayed slumped in the gaming chair long after they left.

Any other evening he'd be considering what to order in for dinner back at the apartment. He'd ordered in from a selection of restaurants every night this week and not tried to stop her leaving early again. Now he understood her deep need for independence, he didn't want to make her feel controlled. He'd long had his independence, but she'd long been denied hers. It riled him more than anything. He loathed controlling bullies like her father. Yet, *her* boundaries around their affair chaffed. He didn't like being told what he could and couldn't do, either. He *wasn't* like that jerk she'd had the affair with. Sante would treat her—a restaurant, a walk through the city, a trip to... anywhere. But she insisted on absolute discretion, determined not to be seen with him outside the office. He knew his annoyance about it was ironic when he was the privacy freak. But he wanted to sit opposite her and take time over their meal. He wanted to dance with her in a club, not just on the patio at the palazzo or in the glasshouse. She would glitter. She always glittered. His pilot Jerome knew they spent the weekends together and while he was discreet, Sante knew it was only a matter of time before others in his office became aware of their routine. Would it matter that much if people did?

Because if they didn't have to be secret, they could go to Paris or Barcelona for a few days—preferably *during* the week because the weekends in Sicily felt sacrosanct. He didn't want to miss having her there.

He heard her humming and smiled, knowing the office was now empty. She'd brought music back into his life, too.

'Were you protecting me from prying questions?' he asked when she sank into the second gaming chair, certain he'd not imagined that hint of proprietary care in her interruption earlier.

She shrugged. 'I know you don't like to share personal things.'

He kept watching her. Waiting.

'No one knows anything about you.' She picked up the controller, selected a game and pressed Play. 'You're a reclusive, elusive genius with no personal details on your website. Not even the name of your company has any obvious connection to you. I had to ask the guys why they wanted to work for you. They all said the same thing.'

'The money.' Sante clicked, selecting his avatar, ready to best her on screen at least.

'You really think your value is only in your bank balance?'

He leaned back in the chair. 'I prefer not to discuss my background because then there will be fewer preconceived judgements or ideas about me and, therefore, my work.'

'You like to let the product speak for itself.'

That had been the money he'd taken and run with. 'It was a means to an end.'

'Freedom. Security. Property.' She leaned forward, eyes narrowing on the screen as they raced. 'So why create this incubator for other genius misfits now?'

'I have too many ideas. I want them to take them off my hands. Personal questions invariably lead to judgement. Someone finds out you were a foster kid, there's automatically the question *why*. What was wrong with me to be in foster care?'

Mia fumbled, accidentally tripping her character. 'You were in foster care?'

Sante hit Pause on the game. 'You really didn't know?'

'How could I?' She tilted her head towards him as she realised. 'You told Dario. He never said anything to me.'

Sante supposed he should be grateful the guy hadn't told the world about his past. '*Sì*.'

She moved forward, turning his face so she could look into his eyes. 'Sante, you can't think anything was wrong with you,' she whispered.

'Don't you wonder what was wrong with you that your father didn't want you?'

'I don't need to wonder. I know. Because I was like my mother, he couldn't stand to look at me. It spiralled down from there.'

'You reminded him of heartbreak. It made him angry.'

'You assume he had a heart to break. I don't think he had one.'

'Maybe not, given how he treated you in life.' He sighed. 'I wonder what it was that I reminded my mother of that made her want to put me in a cardboard box and leave me at a church gate.'

'Sante…' She stared at him, clearly shocked. 'You don't have to tell me anything else. Some things hurt too much to be stirred up and discussed.' She suddenly blurted, 'I don't need to know your past to know what kind of person you are now.'

He stiffened.

'Seriously, you're no mystery to me,' she added. 'There's plenty I know about you. You don't have to open up to me or anything.'

Sante smiled ruefully, appreciating that she was trying hard not to pry and accepting his reticence instead.

'What do you think you know?' He leaned back.

'I'm not talking about knowing you in the biblical sense.' Her smile was tinged with sadness. 'I'm talking about knowing you here.' She reached across and pressed her palm on his chest, right over his heart. 'You're quiet. You like to watch and observe.'

'How astute, Captain Obvious.'

'But you can't quite separate yourself completely.' She ignored his dryness. 'You care about people. You care about your coders and creatives. You care about Adele and Bruno. And your neighbours. You can't stop yourself caring completely. I know you're loyal. You're willing to put yourself at risk to help another. Especially someone you care about.'

His eyes widened. He didn't have relationships based in anything emotional. Dario was right; he was transactional. Furthermore, his interactions with others were invariably temporary. Which was how he liked it. Even this now with Mia was only temporary and only sexual. But she was arguing differently. Wrongly.

'You're aware of the needs of others and you're receptive to change.'

'Is this the open-door policy?' he drawled, trying not to take any of this seriously.

'And the shared lunch, yes, it is. But it's also phoning your neighbours to make sure they were okay in the storm.'

'That was just being…' He cleared his throat. 'It's better for my property if the ones next door are well maintained.'

'It was giving "kind human." One who has connections even when he pretends to himself that he doesn't. I don't need to know everything about you to know that you're a decent person.'

'You're a blind optimist. I have faults, too.'

'Oh yeah, heaps.'

He cocked his head, suddenly amused. 'Such as…'

'Ego,' she chuckled. 'Impatience.' She leaned close to whisper. 'Insecurity.'

'Is that a fault?'

'It can be. When it stops you believing you can do things.'

'You think I lack self-belief?' he scoffed.

'No. I think you lack belief in *others*. That they'll truly be there for you.'

He stilled. 'Maybe you're projecting.'

'Probably. Maybe we have more in common than we'd first have thought.'

'More than an insatiable sex drive?' he teased but he didn't really feel like laughing.

She shook her head.

And weirdly, her lack of intrusion loosened his tongue. She cared about everyone. She was caring enough *not* to ask even though he knew she was curious. He wanted her to know why he wouldn't ever…couldn't ever…have anything more than something like this.

'My early childhood was okay.' He found himself reassuring her. 'I mean, I wasn't wanted by my birth parents. I was found in a box and after a night in hospital went straight into the system. My first foster family already had an older child but then they'd had a baby pass away, so at first I was…' He sighed. 'I was a gift, I guess. But when I was four, my foster mother unexpectedly got pregnant with a real gift. Twins. That meant it was a high-risk pregnancy and she needed to rest a lot and I didn't really understand. I was just…'

Mia's eyes widened. 'A *child*.'

'I came home from nursery school and found my bags packed.'

'They couldn't get help for your foster mother—she had no family support?'

'I guess I wasn't really part of that family.' He'd been with them almost five years and then there'd been *nothing*.

'That was a huge betrayal, Sante. I'm so sorry.'

Sì, Mia knew what it was like to be completely uprooted and forced to go to a place where you weren't welcome. That was the only reason he kept talking. She was one of the few people in the world who would actually understand.

'I didn't last long at the next placement. They'd told me that if I caused trouble, I'd have to move. I ran away, thinking they'd send me back to my first home.'

'But that didn't happen.'

There were rational reasons for difficult decisions, but there was core rejection that couldn't be healed. Nothing to be said to assuage it. Mia looked at him—her expression open. She could be so full of joie de vivre but on the flip side, deeply considerate. And compassionate.

'Did you get placed with another foster family after you ran away?'

'I was at the third home for a few years. They had several foster children. Very strict foster father. He was an athletics coach. He had high expectations of himself, his wife and all of us.'

'Expectations that you would have met. You won that sports scholarship to Dario's school.'

All-rounder scholarship, actually—the academics had been the clincher more than the sporting strength, but he wasn't in the mood to brag.

'I know. So his routines didn't damage me. I could handle the intensity. He wanted to make something of us. We were nothing, but we wouldn't always be nothing because he would help us get there but we had to work for it.'

'He told you that you were nothing?'

'It was five-mile runs before breakfast. Weight training. Things were withheld unless you hit your daily targets.'

'Things?'

'Food. Rest. You had to keep pushing.'

'Oh, Sante.' She looked stricken. 'It was abuse.'

She immediately saw what he hadn't realised for too long.

'I was lucky,' he muttered. 'He set the challenge and I wouldn't give him the satisfaction of beating me. But I'd been blessed with a strong enough body to be able to endure it. But Luca wasn't.' He dropped his gaze. 'He'd been there about a year and he struggled. One weekend I was away at a meet. The foster father would normally come on those trips. He liked to watch me win. It was good because it gave the others a break from his supervision. But my foster mother was unwell and he had to stay home. Which made him frustrated and when he was frustrated, he would blow the whistle and demand more effort. Other times I was able to distract him—ask him to spot me for my weights routines. Ask his advice. Flatter him.'

'You played him to protect the others,' she said. 'But that time you weren't there. What happened to Luca?'

'They assessed him at the hospital. Aside from the broken ribs there were all kinds of overuse injuries. They shut down the home. The foster father was charged with cruelty. But I was the success story. He used me as the model to prove his strategy worked. The social workers challenged me. Why hadn't I said anything? Or done anything to stop him? She said I was selfish because I could do it and show off and that I was as bad as he was.'

'Sante, you know that wasn't fair.'

He bent his head. 'She was right.'

'You were a *child*. You tried to protect the others by taking the attention of your foster father the one way you could. Sante, *none* of it was your fault.' She paused. 'What happened to Luca?'

'I never saw him again.' He glanced up. 'I was sent to a group home and a new school. The principal there helped me apply to that school in Wales.'

'Dario's school. It was supposed to have changed your life.'

'Get me a full ride to an elite university, *sì*. Make connections with the right people. The principal was delighted for me.'

'Were you delighted?'

'You know how hard it is to leave the place you've lived your whole life and go somewhere wildly different. When you don't speak the language all that well…'

'It's hard,' she said. 'Especially without anyone to support you.'

'I met Dario,' he muttered.

Her brother had become a friend. The one person he

could speak in his own language with. They'd joked about creating apps that would make them billions. But Sante had always been serious. Dario was as smart. As sporty. Idealistic. He'd been a friend and competitor. Dario had wanted to do big things, to make a difference. He'd been a damn idealist. But he'd had a backstop. He'd had a family. Money. Entitlement. He could *afford* to be idealistic. For Sante it had only been about *survival*. Of course he'd wanted to make money. He'd wanted to create security for *himself*. He'd wanted personal freedom. Never to have to perform for anyone again. Never be told what he could or couldn't do. Never feel trapped and helpless. Never have to suck up to powerful people or feel as if he were the change in a transaction. Never rely on anyone—never make the mistake of letting anyone close ever again.

Certainly not the baby sister of the guy he'd felt betrayed him most.

'But then you had the accident,' Mia said softly after a while. 'You tried to help Dario. You just ran the opposite way to which help came.'

'I failed,' Sante said harshly.

'You still tried. That matters, Sante.'

No. Failure sucked. It had ended that friendship. He would fail her at some point. He couldn't sustain relationships. Once again, he'd failed to protect someone he'd come to feel close to. He wouldn't be close to anyone again.

'For what it's worth, Dario shut everyone out. Even me,' Mia said.

Dario had believed Sante had abandoned him when he was hurt. Abandonment was one of the worst things that could happen to a person. He would never have done it. That Dario believed he had just said it all.

He was blamed again—everything about the accident deemed to be his fault. Going to the music festival had been Dario's idea. Sante had never been to one and he'd thought it would be fun. But Dario's father had blamed him. The police had shamed him. He'd taken one look at the principal's face and known to withdraw as a student before he was expelled. As he was seventeen they didn't bother to try stopping him. That had ended the scholarship offers for university.

He'd always been discarded. If something or someone better had come along. Or if there was a problem—if *he* caused any problems. For any arbitrary reason. Any trouble and Sante was blamed first. Judgement lingered. Assumptions, negative expectations, were what stuck with him, never people.

The moment anyone found out about his past, their perceptions shifted. His achievements were marvelled at—as if somehow it was a miracle that someone like him could do anything beyond the norm. He wasn't letting anyone reject him again. He took control of everything. Always.

'After the accident you came back to Italy?' Mia asked.

'Like you I took jobs that included food and accommodation so I could save everything. Worked through the night on my app.'

'You must have been exhausted.'

'There wasn't any other choice.'

'You could have taken my father's money.' She smiled sadly. 'I know you didn't. You're not big on taking help from anyone.'

'That wasn't help,' he said gruffly.

She nodded. 'It's hard to ask for help, let alone accept it, when you've been let down by people in the past and almost everyone let you down.' She fiddled with the controller, her voice going husky. 'Until Adele. She's been constant.'

'I needed someone to take the phone calls and do the admin. She stays because I pay her well and she has financial stresses that require her to remain. Her loyalty isn't personal.'

'You know that's neither fair nor true. She cares about you. She just knows better than to *let* you see it. Her desperation to get me to handle the office wasn't just about Bruno. It was for you, too.' She lifted those lashes and gazed at him, emotion blooming in her blue eyes. 'And I bet you've never told her about your past. So it's not pity, Sante. You know that and it goes both ways. That's why you've been helping her by paying for Bruno's new specialist.'

'You know about that?' He frowned. 'Does *she* know about that?'

He'd pulled some strings—made a donation. Because Mia was right. Adele had been constant and he'd been compelled to help even if it was only in the one way he could—financially.

'Of course not. I guessed when she told me they'd gotten a referral to the top guy in Rome. I knew I was right.'

'Want to lean on her to accept a cook and cleaner as well?'

'Leave it with me.' Mia nodded but her smile was sad. 'The reason you don't have personal photos is because you don't actually have any, isn't it?'

'Why does that bother you so much?' But she was

right. No family. No photos. 'The photo on my file is like a police mugshot. But it doesn't matter. I don't want reminders of that time.'

'Did you ever try to find your biological parents?'

'There were no DNA matches in any databases at the time and I don't want to find out now. They didn't want me. I don't want them.' He fully imagined the worst.

'You don't have to have DNA answers to know who you are, Sante. You're a good person.'

'Am I? My genetics might be flawed. I might have inheritable diseases in my body or brain—undesirable personality traits or—'

'We all have messy genes. We're not clones of our parents. You're still you. You're in charge of your destiny—you've proven that beyond doubt. But I'll admit you're not normal, Sante,' she said. 'You're *exceptional* in so many ways.'

'Mia—'

'I stand by what I know,' she said softly. 'You're aware of others. You help. You *care*.'

'Don't start thinking I'm something I'm not,' he muttered, rejecting her innate positivity. 'I'll only disappoint you, Mia.'

'Lots of things in life are a disappointment.' She shrugged but then shot him a loyal look that lanced. 'But you never will be.'

CHAPTER ELEVEN

MIA WALKED ON her lunch breaks—a half hour of sunshine and solitude. Sometimes she checked in with Adele—who'd finally accepted the additional support that Sante had been desperate to supply—but mostly she processed the time with Sante, trying to lock it into her memory so she could savour every sensation. Somehow, two weeks had passed since that first weekend in Sicily. The time had passed in a dreamy blur of sizzling sweet torture in the office before the too-quick delights of nighttime—dining in his apartment, debating over the best songs of the century, destroying each other on the gaming console before teasing higher stakes games in bed. The weekends in Sicily were slower, lazier, decadent. She caught up on the sleep she'd missed through the week while Sante worked in the garden or read. He still worked so hard so she liked to play with him—putting on music, dancing naked in the glasshouse, reading, eating…and spending hours in bed. Her adjustment to helicopter flights, fridges full of delicacies and walking into perfect homes prepared by discreet staff was shamelessly effortless. Every aspect of this lifestyle was utter luxury but her most favourite thing was the attention from *him*. Sante spoilt her in the best possible way—with his focus and time. It was so good she was struggling about missing it even before their affair was ended. Because this *was* an affair and she reminded herself of the fact daily.

She didn't like to open up emotionally. It was simpler to live lightly, never scratch beneath the superficial. She enjoyed a job, or a new place but moved on before anything went wrong—but she kept in touch with many people, revisited places. She just was always careful not to stay too long.

Sante preferred not to open up as well—he retreated to his sanctuary, not letting anyone past his guard and given what he'd been through, she didn't blame him. And while he'd opened up with her, it was partly only because of their shared past. His isolation increasingly bothered her. She remembered that summer back at her father's estate when she'd been jealous of and fascinated by her brother's best friend. She remembered hearing their banter, their competitiveness, their laughter.

For all this time since, Dario had kept the sad facts of Sante's childhood private and now Mia couldn't understand why he'd believed their father about Sante's behaviour after the accident—why he would accept that Sante hadn't just abandoned him but taken money to stay away. Their friendship hadn't just been severed, but Dario still seethed with resentment. Her brother's awful injuries still caused him pain and it must've been hard to see his former friend succeeding back when he was so broken. But Dario had worked stupidly hard to 'catch up' on the time he'd missed. He *still* worked stupidly hard. So did Sante. Initially, they'd created complementary products but despite their past closeness, 'doesn't play well with others' was stamped across both their report cards now.

It shouldn't be. They'd been on the same team once, and while Sante mightn't agree, he was effectively building himself a team here in Rome. He and Dario had so much in common. If they could clear the air maybe they'd see they *weren't* each other's nemesis. Knowing the truth about Sante—that he hadn't taken any money—might lighten her brother up. And hiding her affair from him felt wrong to Mia. Because this was more than a physical thing. She *cared* about Sante and she didn't want either him or her brother to be so *alone*. Maybe she could make a difference to them. Maybe she could bring *them* together.

Impulsively, Mia pulled out her phone.

'Mia?' Dario abruptly answered on the third ring. 'What's up—is everything okay?'

He sounded so concerned—did he think she'd only phone if something was wrong?

'Everything's fine.' Her pulse accelerated. 'I just thought it had been a while since we caught—'

'I figured you've been working on board somewhere sunny,' Dario said.

'I was, but I've taken a temporary position in Rome. Funny thing, actually.' She squeezed her eyes shut and went for it. 'I'm working for Sante Trovato's tech incubator.'

For a moment there was no response. Then she heard a door slam.

'Can you repeat that please, Mia?' Dario's voice suddenly sounded much nearer, much softer, much more serious.

Mia immediately overcompensated—smiling to inject lightness into her voice. 'I'm working with Sante Trovato. You remember—'

'Of course I remember.'

Mia tried to soften her own tension and remain calm. 'I didn't realise when I took the job that he—'

'Mia!' Dario groaned. 'Listen to *me*,' her brother added urgently. 'You need to stand up and walk out of there right now.'

'I can't do that.'

'Yes, you can. He has no hold over you, Mia. He's bad news.'

But Sante did have a hold—on her heart. 'If you really want to know, I'm involved with him.'

'*What?*' Dario's question cracked like a whip.

It was just like the way their father asked whenever she'd screwed up in his eyes. Because that was what she did, right? Messed up. Was too impetuous. Was *stupid*.

'Are you sleeping with him?' Dario almost choked. 'Why would you fall for his false charm?'

Which showed how much Dario actually knew because Sante was *not* charming. He was guarded and prickly with *everyone*.

'No, Mia,' Dario added. 'You know he's a user. You know he'll just take what he wants, then leave. No goodbye. No backwards glance. He's only interested in what he can get out of people and then he's gone.'

Mia would have agreed with that assessment only a couple weeks ago but working with him, being with him, she'd gotten to truly know him. 'You're wrong, Dario. He didn't abandon you that night. And he never took money from Dad. He cares about—'

'About *his* needs,' Dario argued. 'He's using you, Mia. It's a cheap double win—he gets what he wants from you *and* he gets at me.'

Cheap. *Sex.* She stiffened at the implication that that was all a man could want from her.

And Dario believed he was the true target in Sante's interest in her—why? Because he was more important? The firstborn with the balls and the brains and thus the title.

Dario got horrible attention from their father, too, but he *was* valued more—he was *wanted* if only to be the heir—and that still hurt.

'Maybe what's going on between him and me has nothing to do with you,' she said.

'It has *everything* to do with me. He wants to score points against me and he's using you to do it.' Dario scoffed again. 'Don't be this naive, Mia.'

Actually, she wasn't. She'd been thriving just fine on her own for the past few years. Travelling, working hard, managing the money she earned. But her brother still didn't think that she was *capable*.

'What do you think is going to happen here, Mia? You can't trust him. I don't want to see you hurt—'

'I won't be,' she defended fiercely. 'And if you met him—'

'That's *never* going to happen.' Dario's disbelief streamed through the phone.

'Not even if I ask?' she murmured. 'Dario?'

There was silence down the phone.

'The only way I'd meet him is on the day he marries you,' Dario said brutally. 'Is that going to happen, Mia?'

'No, because that's not what I want,' she shot back. 'You know I *like* my independence. There's nothing more important to me. I just thought *you* should know that he's not the awful man you—'

'He's *worse* and—'

'Can't you trust my judgement?' she interrupted. 'Can't you consider this for me?'

Dario sighed heavily. 'Mia, I can't. I know you. You're so like Mum—too generous, too impetuous. You dive headlong into situations that don't serve you—'

He broke off and she heard him cursing beneath his breath.

Right. He thought she was screwing up her life. He was tarnishing her with their mother's failings just as their father had. Mia's anger sparked. 'Maybe I'm like her in daring to enjoy—'

'Mum was an *addict*, Mia. You don't know—'

'*You* don't give me any credit for being able to understand anything, but *you're* the one who doesn't understand subtleties and shades of grey and that reality might not be as binary as you'd like it to be. I'm *not* a child anymore. And I'm *not* Mum. I'm capable of evaluating evidence and making rational decisions—'

'Sleeping with Sante Trovato isn't a rational decision. Please, Mia. He's using you.'

Using her to hurt Dario. Using her just for convenient sex. Dario couldn't consider otherwise. *Mia* couldn't possibly be wanted for anything other than her connections or her body.

'I'm sorry,' she muttered, and she was because she heard the pain in her brother's voice. 'I shouldn't have talked to you about it. I shouldn't have tried to—' She broke off with a jerky inhalation. 'Don't worry, okay? I *am* leaving here soon and it will be over so just forget I ever said anything about it.'

She ended the call before he could reply and shoved her phone into her pocket. She was in control of herself here, wasn't she? But Dario's cynicism didn't seed doubt, it made her fully face her own actions. Her own feelings.

She *had* been impetuous in starting the affair with Sante and she was under no illusions that *she* had started it. It should've been a short-term fun fling—not heavy or serious. She'd not meant to feel anything deeply for him. But now she saw she'd not been daring to enjoy physical pleasure with him; she'd dared her *heart*. She just hadn't realised it. And now it was too late.

She *liked* him. She more than liked him. And she didn't want this to end.

But Sante had never hinted that he'd want anything more and it was insane to think he would given they'd only been together a few weeks. The truth was he hated her father and he hated her brother and he couldn't overcome that past any more than Dario could. Her wishing for a different future was pointless. They *would* end.

She was a fool for having given in to her desire in the first place. But she couldn't regret it.

Heart aching, she turned back to walk towards the office. The streets were crowded with both tourists and workers and she was carried along with them back towards Sante's building. She was relieved to get inside and into the cool stairwell. She heard voices just above—others climbing the stairs ahead of her.

'…they both stayed late the other night. You know they're always last to leave so who knows what happens when we're all gone.'

Mia stilled. There was someone on the landing above; despite talking quietly their words carried down the empty stairwell towards her.

'Carla went in the helicopter the other day and saw the last few flight logs. Apparently, Mia's been a passenger on the weekend trips to Sicily. She's not been in the office the last couple Fridays. You know they're not working all weekend.'

Horrified, she pressed back against the wall. They were talking about *her*. And Sante.

'No *way*,' Davide scoffed. 'I don't believe it.'

'You watch—you'll see the way she looks at him.'

Shame slithered over Mia's skin.

'No!' Davide was in full disbelief. 'They're total opposites. He wouldn't. She's far too—'

Mia didn't hear what Davide said but the men's laughter streamed down the stairwell. Amazed. Amused. *Derisive.*

'He's a guy, isn't he? He'd totally do it. Wouldn't you?'

'Yeah, but—'

Mia closed her eyes and covered her face with her hands, blocking out the rest of what they said. She'd been *obvious* and the colleagues whom she thought respected her clearly didn't. They were discussing her as a sexual *option*. Staying working here now was untenable. She couldn't—knowing they were watching her. *Mocking* her. She simply couldn't live through the humiliation of an exposed workplace affair.

But their *laughter* shook her. It hurt more than her brother's concerns. Dario believed Sante was using her—that he didn't really want her. But these guys knew Sante far better that Dario now did and they saw the truth. *Mia* was the misfit in the relationship. She was too…*something*. She didn't need to know exactly what—it was always the same. Too much in one way, too lacking in another. She wouldn't ever be considered a serious match for Sante Trovato.

And it was devastating.

* * *

Sante restlessly prowled around the open-plan area knowing he was freaking the coders out but he couldn't stop pacing. Mia wasn't yet back from her lunchtime walk. She wasn't normally gone for this long and he couldn't help lingering—watching, waiting, his nerves shredding more by the second. He wasn't even able to focus enough to have a crack at the game of the week for her league table. Because he'd done something impulsive. He'd made a Mia-like plan. Or so he hoped. He'd wanted to do something nice with her—*for* her—and the trip he'd booked definitely ticked those boxes. They'd have to take a couple days more away from the office, but she'd not had a holiday since starting here and he couldn't remember the last time he'd had a holiday that wasn't simply a trip to his estate. Nor could he remember the last time he'd felt this nervous.

It was a good idea. It was. She'd love it. She would smile and her cheeks would flush and they would have fun.

The door opened and Mattia, the property junior, walked in with Davide, one of the coders. Disappointed, Sante turned back and kept prowling round the room. Ten minutes passed before the door opened again.

Sante stilled. Mia looked pale and her eyes were downcast as she went to her desk. There was no smile or gentle greeting to anyone she walked past—which was weird. He immediately headed back to his office via her corner.

'Do you have a minute, Mia?' He nodded towards his door.

She didn't answer but after a moment rose and followed him into his office. She didn't close his door behind her. She didn't meet his eye. Sante took in her visible attempt to hold herself together. She was quite literally clasping her hands tightly in front of her. While they weren't hands-on in the office, they were friendly. They made eye contact.

'Are you okay?' he asked quietly, moving closer to her.

'Of course.' She still didn't meet his eye; instead, she glanced at the window.

'I, uh…' Awkward discomfort licked through him. He was so unpractised, he didn't know where to begin. 'I've booked some tickets. For a concert. In London.'

Not just any tickets. Most expensive available.

'*London?*' She looked at him then and her eyes widened. '*A concert? What?*'

'We'd have to take—'

'Sante,' she interrupted. 'Is this a work thing?'

He blinked. No, it wasn't. What did that matter?

She bit her lip. 'You know the rules…'

Did those rules still matter? Really?

Her wariness raised red flags in his head. He'd wanted to take her away. He'd booked for the band who sang her favourite songs. It was the final concert of their world tour and the timing was insane and he'd thought she would *love* it. That they both would—she'd liked dancing with him in the palazzo… But now Mia's creamy skin paled, even her full lips whitened. She almost looked ill. Was it London that spooked her? She would have friends there from when she grew up. Others from her aristocratic background. The school she went to. The jobs she'd worked.

She checked the window again. Sante glanced at it, too, and saw a couple of coders walk past towards the kitchenette—both of whom looked in.

Sante turned back to Mia. Now her cheeks were mottled crimson and she actually took a step back. *'Please*, Sante.'

Mia—his lovely, enthusiastic, effervescent, loud Mia, *whispered*.

She didn't want to be heard discussing anything personal with him. She didn't want to be *seen* with him in a personal capacity. And if she couldn't handle being seen with him here, there's no way she'd agree to be in the VIP section of one of the world's biggest concert arenas, rubbing shoulders with celebrities and the toffs she went to school with.

'We can't talk about this now,' she added.

They didn't need to talk about it. Her answer was obvious. It was going to be no. And he didn't want to hear it. He *couldn't*. She'd said they came from different worlds and she didn't want them to mix. All of a sudden he wasn't Sante Trovato, billionaire. But Sante, the foundling— unwanted, parentage unknown, *problematic*.

'Right,' he said brusquely.

He was a fool for plotting this—for ever imagining she would walk out with him anywhere public. She would never want anyone to know—certainly not her brother. Hell, Sante hadn't been to a concert since the night of their accident, and there would never be any way he could make any of this work.

'Sante…' she muttered. 'Please—'

'Sorry—oh, am I interrupting?' Paolo paused in the doorway.

'No, come in.' Sante jerked his chin at the man and flatly dismissed her. 'We're done here, right, Mia?'

She escaped wordlessly.

His pulse pounded. She'd rejected him. She'd not

needed to say a word; he'd read it in her eyes. It was his mistake. He didn't want to be a secret. Not her source of shame. He'd felt so much shame in his life. And now he'd exposed himself—made himself *vulnerable* to that rejection. He'd not allowed that possibility in *years* but he'd just let her slice the ground from beneath his feet and he was *falling*—

'What is it, Paolo?' he asked harshly.

Desperate for distraction, Sante fell on the info that Paolo had brought in with him. A contact had just informed him about a property coming to market in Monaco. That sounded good. Sante had been considering acquiring one there.

Breathing hard, Sante nodded decisively. He'd go see it for himself. Make the decision on *full* information. This was important. Work was the constant. Work was the only thing that mattered. He would head there. *Now.*

CHAPTER TWELVE

MIA COMPLETELY UNNECESSARILY sent a document to the farthest printer simply to have reason to get away from her desk. As she walked back, she used peripheral vision to see Sante still intensely talking with Paolo in his office. She let her glance sweep the room and saw Davide watching her. She dropped her lashes and went straight back to her desk.

He knew. Which meant they *all* knew. She was such a fool to have let this happen. She desperately needed to talk to Sante *privately*—as in off-site—so she could explain exactly why she'd not wanted to talk about his plans here. She'd thought he would understand given he'd been empathetic about what had happened with Oliver. And what had he meant by tickets to a concert in *London*? Who and what and *why* had he done that? She *ached* to know now but ten minutes ago she'd been feeling trash with Dario pitying her, hearing those guys laughing about her and she'd just needed him to stop.

He'd done more than that. He'd shut down. His dismissal—that they were *done*? That had sounded final.

Five minutes after she'd left Sante's office, Paolo exited—Sante just behind him. He walked past her, jacket and bag in hand. Mia didn't look up; she couldn't. She checked the schedule but nothing new had been added. She heard the bang as the main door closed behind him but she couldn't chase after him given the curious gazes of the coders.

Instead, she faked being busy—clicking windows on her computer screen as if her life depended on it and overthinking everything. She was totally thrown by that invitation—it was thoughtful and generous and what had he meant by it?

She willed the workday to end. Willed Sante to return. Wished she could get to a space where she could be alone and think. But she couldn't just leave. She couldn't go away to London with him and have everyone know it.

An hour later a message pinged on the company-wide message board.

Gone to investigate a property. Back soon. Keep pushing *S.

It was more information than Sante usually offered the team when going away but Mia felt hurt that there was no message directly to her inbox. Nor her phone. She braved up and sent him a text—saying they needed to talk, asking when he'd be back.

Two days later she was still waiting on a reply.

Three days later she'd accepted the reality. She'd thought he'd get in touch and while he responded to work emails and updates—briefly—his message was clear. He didn't want *her*. Those tersely worded work instructions made her feel worse. He sent them only because he'd *had* to. Otherwise, he would've severed all ties—on a personal level he had, no texts, no calls. He'd walked out and never looked back.

That was what he'd done to Dario after the accident. What he'd done with that school. And with his foster placement. It was how he dealt—he walked away, stayed away, stayed silent.

'Are you okay, Mia?'

Mia glanced up and saw Valerio quietly standing near. She couldn't even interpret his question—whether he, too, knew and was asking with gossipy intent or whether he genuinely cared.

'I'm fine, thank you,' she lied.

She wasn't fine. She was furious. And even though she knew it was horrible to simply disappear from people's lives, at 11 am on the third day of Sante's absence she closed down her computer, shoved her spare blouse into her bag and walked out of the office without a word to anyone.

As soon as she was out in the bright sunshine she grabbed her phone and tapped the screen. Her call was answered almost immediately.

'Adele?' She checked. 'I'm so sorry.'

Sante's thundering pulse deafened him to everything. Nothing within him would work properly. He couldn't even get it together enough to bother walking around the stunning building overlooking a vast coastline. He just stood in front of it and felt like crap. Alone. Again. Again. Again.

He'd gone straight to the airport—so desperate to escape he'd actually flown commercial. First class, but still, it was cramped and crowded. He'd walked through the apartment in Monaco and gone straight back to the airport. Restless as hell. He'd felt a biting drive for space and distance and so he'd gotten onto another flight; this time Melbourne, Australia. He'd spent more than fifteen hours in the air all up. Which gave him plenty of time to think. To *stew*.

He'd thought he'd visit his favourite properties, remind himself what he liked, what he'd achieved, what was most important to him. All that had happened was that he'd wished Mia was with him. At every moment. Every place. He'd wanted her with him. He'd *missed* her. And he was an idiot because she didn't want to be seen with him. She didn't want to talk with him in private. Never wanted to leave his apartment in Rome or the estate in Sicily. Half the time she didn't want to stay in his bed the entire night. She wanted to have sex with him, but anything more?

It hurt. Especially because he knew damned well she was an 'all in' person—with impulsive warmth, generous with her self, her soul. It wasn't hedonism—there was a deliberate direction in her choices. She'd turned her full-bore attention to him but it had been *confined*. She'd wanted him but only if it was *quiet*. And he was furious with her for that. Furious with himself for *still* wanting more. And his fury surged—unabated, unanswered. He wanted to know *why*—to hear the trash reasons from her mouth. To watch her eyes as she answered. And he needed to tell her how much *she* bothered him.

He'd made a mistake in running away from the fight. He needed to have the fight with her to be able to *forget*.

It was days before he got to her apartment. There was no answer when he rang her doorbell. He glanced at his watch and cursed his idiocy. She would be at work by now. The emails had still been coming but she'd not offered anything personal other than that one text he'd not replied to.

He stalked through the office, stopping at her empty desk and glancing around. Why wasn't she here already? The main door opened and he whirled to face it. Freezing when he saw who'd entered.

'What are you doing here?' he muttered huskily. 'You can't be here.'

Adele merely raised her eyebrows at him.

'I thought you were taking three *months*, not three weeks,' Sante added.

'Apparently, my fussing is driving Bruno up the wall and he'll do better with a break from me. The specialist you got for him is amazing, the cleaner is amazing and his best friend is dropping in. So he's in good spirits and I'm needed here.'

Why? Sante's chest felt hollowed out by a spoon. 'Where's Mia?'

Adele got busy unpacking her bag at Mia's desk and wouldn't look at him. 'I'll be in the office three days—'

'And Mia the other two?' Sante interrupted.

Adele straightened and looked him in the eye. 'No, Sante. Mia's gone.'

He shook his head. 'She wouldn't have done that. She wouldn't let you down.'

'*She's* not the one who's let me down.' Adele paused.

His heart thudded and instinctively he pressed his lips together. She was scolding him—about the only person he'd take it from.

'Mia's a generous soul,' Adele added quietly. 'I'd hoped you might see that.'

Of course he had. The problem was he wanted too *much* of her generosity.

'She was right about you,' Adele added.

Meaning what, exactly? But Adele didn't say more.

Sante drew breath, softening stiff muscles enough to be able to speak. 'Where can I find her?'

The older woman sat at her desk and didn't answer.

'So, you know we're…' He trailed off.

'Everyone knows you're together,' Adele said calmly. 'Isn't that part of the problem?'

He frowned. Everyone? Already? In his head that had been inevitable, but while he didn't care, the thought bothered Mia. A lot. 'Did someone say something?'

Adele looked at him like he was an imbecile. He frowned. Had they said something off? Was that why Mia had been so uncomfortable that day? Then why hadn't she said anything to *him*?

Because he'd not given her a proper chance to. And she *had* said something—she'd said they couldn't talk *here*. In his office with all its windows and open-plan space. And he really was a fool. He'd taken her hesitation so badly—so *personally*. He'd immediately assumed her reluctance was regarding his invitation. He'd been so *insecure*. So he'd backed off.

He'd disappeared and then *she'd* disappeared. And wasn't that what he'd wanted? He'd known his silence would hurt her. He'd known his *disappearance* would drive her away. He'd been horrible because he'd felt not good enough for her and couldn't handle the prospect of her rejection. Now he felt even more horrible because driving her away wasn't what he'd wanted at all. It was the complete *opposite* of what he wanted. He'd been such a coward. He'd hurt himself. And he was still so damned insecure he didn't know how *badly* he'd hurt her.

But he did know that Mia was empathetic and loving. When she'd first realised who he was, she'd sided with Dario's version of their past with almost blind loyalty because she loved her brother deeply. The magnitude of Mia's emotions had always attracted Sante—he wanted her to feel deeply for him, too. For him most of all. He wanted every ounce of her generosity—both body and heart. He'd wanted it so much he'd gotten scared and pushed her away instead of speaking up. But Mia needed love, too—the certainty of that body-and-soul kind of love. She'd never had it and she feared rejection as much as he did. She walked out when she felt that she'd been too much—but she could *never* be too much for him.

'I get that you're angry with me. *I'm* angry with me,' Sante said to the woman who'd been better to him than almost anyone. Because now he understood that she'd chosen Mia to help, oh *so* deliberately. 'I screwed up but I can't fix it if I don't know where to find her.'

Adele looked up, her gaze serious. 'Do you actually want to fix it?'

A desperate, desolate ache swept through him. 'More than anything,' he admitted hoarsely. 'But she's the one who needs to hear why. Though admittedly, I might need help with how.' He leaned against the wall and ran his hand through his hair. 'Please, Adele, I know you know where she is. Will you tell me?'

CHAPTER THIRTEEN

ADELE TOLD HIM a little more information—by the end, Sante was feeling small but hopeful. Also desperate. Also grateful to the woman—she'd been more loyal than he deserved and she'd put up with more of his flaky behaviour than she should have.

The only person to call him out on it up to now had been Mia.

But he'd apologised and gone straight back to the damned airport. The irony was too much as he boarded another endurance-test flight. Mia had gone even farther than him—not to Australia, but New Zealand. Of course she had. Which meant it would be almost another day before he could see her. Adele had given him her new number and the address she was staying at. He didn't phone ahead; face-to-face was the only way. He needed to see her; hopefully, make her listen somehow.

She was staying in a small hotel on the waterfront of a suburb not too far from central Auckland. Sante went straight from the airport, knocked on the door of her unit and got no reply. Frustrated, he stepped back and sucked in a breath. He'd wait. He'd sit on one of the beachside benches by the water where all the people walked their dogs along the sand. He'd wait and watch her door for as long as it took.

But that was where he found her. Sitting on one of the beachside benches, watching the dogs gambolling over the sand. For a split second he thought he was hallucinating because it was the Mia he knew from Rome—wearing the same blouse and skirt from the day he'd met her. It was as if she'd been plucked from there and transported here in a blink. No pastry, though. No spark. No smile.

'Mia?' he barely muttered as he walked up to her.

She glanced up and a shocked expression flashed on her face. '*No.*'

He wasn't hallucinating, then. His entire body weakened and he sank to the other end of the bench. 'Mia—'

'I don't have time to talk to you right now. I have an interview to get to.'

'Job interview?'

She nodded, crushing his lungs.

He dragged in a breath. 'Well, can I give you a lift there?'

Reproach flashed in her eyes. 'No, thanks.'

'Can I walk with you?'

'No.' She shook her head. 'I'm not making this mistake again.'

Then he would wait right here until she returned.

But she hesitated, staying perched on the edge of the seat. 'What do you want?'

'To talk to you.'

'You could have talked to me anytime in these last few days.'

Sì. 'I was travelling.'

'You could've called from your plane.'

'You've changed your number and I wanted to look you in the eyes when I talked to you.'

She didn't move and he watched the blue deepen. A small bubble of hope flickered through his blood.

'What did you want to say?' she muttered.

All those hours in the air and he still didn't have it straight. Didn't know how or where to start something so vitally important.

'Adele told me you overheard a couple of our guys talking in the stairwell,' he huffed.

She tensed. 'I don't—'

'I talked to Davide about it.'

'You *what*?'

'Davide said he'd told Mattia you were far too good for me. I think you missed that bit. They were laughing about *my* unsuitability for you. And he's right, by the way.'

'What?' Her whisper was inaudible.

'I shouldn't have tried to talk about the trip to you at work. I was nervous and I made a mess of it. You'd told me you wanted to keep our relationship quiet at work but I started feeling as if you didn't want anyone to know because you were ashamed of me.'

'*What?*' That time, her voice was like a whip crack.

Sante almost smiled but the distress in her eyes smote his heart. He really had been a fool. 'Mia...'

'No.'

Mia couldn't do this. She couldn't believe he'd spoken to Davide—of course the guy had spun it that way. Ordinarily she'd be more humiliated only *nothing* could overwhelm the agony she was already suffering this second.

Sante looked *outrageously* amazing and she couldn't stop staring, drinking in every detail. His tan had deepened and his hair was messier than usual, the curling ends utterly roguish. Even in casual trousers, heavy tee and soft leather boat shoes he quietly screamed wealth. He looked as if he'd spent the past week lounging on a private super yacht. Maybe he had been; what would she know given his complete *silence*? They'd had *weeks* of intense intimacy and he'd just left. She'd made a massive mistake in getting involved with him. She'd thought they could have a small secret fling—that there would be no real consequences—but she'd had so *much* to lose.

Once again she'd wanted more from someone who didn't want to give to her. Once again she'd been an 'amusement' only to become an annoyance—someone to be sent away, or simply avoided. But that wasn't the worst of it. The worst was that he'd taken her *heart*—and all her hopes and dreams—with him.

She made herself stand. He immediately rose and she realised her mistake. He was so tall and so handsome, he didn't just block her path, he dazzled her.

'I've been a coward, Mia,' he muttered. 'But you need to know that I will follow you. I will fight for you. I will face my own stupid fears for you because they've been stopping me…'

Mia froze, desperately wanting to believe him, but she knew Sante never stayed for a fight—not a *personal* one. He just stepped back—unwilling to put himself on the line, and she almost understood that given how rough he'd had it in the past. And her own hurt rose in an un-stoppable wave. 'You just *disappeared*.'

'So you left.'

'I'll never stay where I'm not truly wanted,' she whispered. 'You of all people should understand that.'

And he did. She realised that was why he'd done it. He'd known just how cruelly that action would strike.

'You're *wanted*,' he said roughly, stepping forward. '*I* want you. And I don't want anyone or anything but you.' His eyes glinted with ferocity. 'I promise you, Mia. I won't walk out on you ever again.'

She shook her head slightly. She couldn't believe him.

'I'm so sorry, Mia.' His voice broke. 'So sorry. Please, *please* forgive me.'

Mia stilled. Sante never stayed for forgiveness, either, and that broke her heart. Did he think he could never get that? Did he think he would always be kicked away after one mistake? Did he think that he needed to protect himself from everything and everyone including *her*?

She desperately summoned some semblance of calm but the tears she'd been trying to stop spilled down her cheeks. She gulped but couldn't suck her sob back. She was in utter chaos.

'Mia.' Suddenly, Sante stepped forward. He gently cupped the back of her head and pressed her forehead to his chest. Instinctively, she clenched her fists and pushed them against his chest. She *wasn't* just falling into his arms. She would keep some distance because this was…this was…

She didn't know what this was. She didn't want to hope. But hope was a boundless thing that ignored reality. She clenched her fists more tightly, still unable to speak.

Sante didn't fight her stiffness; he didn't try to press her close. He lightly cradled the back of her head, gently stroking her hair while *she* hid her face in his shirt. Because her tears now streamed.

'I'm not letting you go. I'm not. I can't. You're mine,' he breathed. 'Or at least, I'm *yours*. Please forgive me,

Mia. Forgive my silence. I freeze. I retreat. I say nothing. It's always been safer that way. But safe isn't living. It's not loving. And I love you so I can't be silent now. I can't walk away from *you*.'

Her fists unfurled and she spread her fingers over his warmth and strength.

'I was such a jerk,' he said. 'I thought you were going to say no and I regressed in an instant.'

'You wanted to do something nice for me but you—'

'Asked you in the office. With the door open. Maybe I wanted to see if you'd say yes anyway or if you'd freeze. I think maybe everything was getting so good that I got scared and I found a way out. I've pushed people away all my life, Mia, before they can push me out. But that wasn't fair on you. My only excuse is that I've never felt this way about anyone and I was fucking terrified. But I'm even more terrified now.'

'Me, too,' she whispered, collapsing against him completely.

Beneath her cheek his chest rose and fell faster as he pulled her closer still.

'I'd talked to Dario,' she admitted. 'He made me doubt—'

'Me?'

'No. Myself and then I heard Davide talking.'

'Our guys think the world of you—'

'It doesn't matter.'

'It does matter. And they do think you're wonderful. You've made the office so much better. You've made my life incredible.' His arms tightened. 'You know I listen to the songs you hum in my car so I feel near you even when I'm not. I scour menus online because dining different every night with you is so much fun. You make every moment sparkle. I went away this week and spent the whole time wishing you were with me. I've never wanted to share anything the way I want to share *everything* with you. You enrich *my* life. You're generous and warm and welcoming,' he muttered. 'You're the most loveable creature on earth and these last few days have been the worst.'

They'd been the worst for her, too.

'I know you're afraid to trust me now and I don't blame you for that, but here's the thing, Mia,' he muttered directly into her ear. 'You're not too much, not for me. You're *perfect* for me.'

Mia trembled.

'Please,' he whispered. 'Be mine. My Mia.'

She lifted her face and saw his expression was utterly intense and determined. 'Oh, Sante—' She lifted her chin and caught his lips with hers.

Passion shot through her in an electrical surge so powerful she could only cling while his hug became so tight she could barely breathe. But it didn't matter. He was back and he was *hers* and she was never, ever letting him go. Fortunately, he clearly wasn't letting her go, either.

'*Mia, Mia, Mia.*' He kissed her breathlessly. 'Can we get to your room? Now?'

She chuckled as her blood fizzed and her brain jumped all over the place.

'I need to cancel the interview,' she babbled. 'It was with an agency. I can't just not turn up.'

He shot her a rueful smile as he took her hand and laced his fingers through hers. She made the quick call as they walked to the room she'd booked at the little hotel. The moment they were inside he turned to her and she threw her arms around his neck. It was with both laughter and tears that they tumbled together onto the bed.

'I've missed you,' he groaned. 'Having you in my arms, by my side, every moment of every day, I have *missed* you.'

Engulfed in joy she fumbled trying to get his tee up before he swore and took over. Getting naked, being together, was everything. But the relief of seeing him again, when she thought she'd lost him forever, was overwhelming. Her hands stilled and her eyes filled and all she could do was stare at him mistily.

'It's okay,' he said, seeing her torn between distress and delight. 'It's okay.' He pulled her close, gently sweeping his hands over her trembling body. 'I'll never leave you again,' he vowed. 'Never ever let you go.'

He tenderly undressed her with gentle slowness, caring, calming her until the heat flowed back into her body. Until she truly believed. And then she moved—she arched towards him, her hands impatient and her mouth hungry. She needed him inside her—to share that ultimate intimacy with him—*now*. 'Sante.'

'I'm here.' As he sank deep inside her, he closed his eyes briefly and his voice hitched. 'Don't leave me again, either.'

'*Never.*' She trailed her hands down his back and pulled him even deeper into her. She never wanted to hurt him. She hadn't understood that she could. But now she knew she had his heart the same way he had hers. 'Love me, Sante.'

'I do. Will. Always.'

They lay together for a long time after, breathlessly whispering words of love and forgiveness, sharing soft, sweet laughter. But he suddenly rose up onto his elbows and gazed into her eyes even more intensely than he had just before.

'What's wrong?'

'Nothing at all.' He swallowed. 'I just…will you marry me?' he asked shakily. 'Preferably as soon as possible?'

'*What?*' Mia's heart stopped and started all over again—at thrice the pace.

'I love you. I want you. I never want to be apart from you again, and I want you to know and believe it, too. I want you to be mine and I want everyone in the whole damned world to know it. I'd be so proud to be your husband, Mia.'

'Isn't it too…' Mia studied the vulnerability in his eyes.

'No. It's not too soon. Not for me,' he whispered. 'I love you.'

He'd just offered the future she'd not yet dared dream of.

'Yes.' But she was so stunned her answer was soundless.

'Was that a yes?' His eyes gleamed.

'Of course yes!' she screamed.

Sante laughed and rolled, flipping her so she was above him. He swept his hands up, cupping her breasts as he gazed up at her adoringly. 'Then let me love you again, my gorgeous fiancée.'

An hour later she still couldn't stop smiling. 'So you want to elope?'

'No. I want a big wedding.'

She yelped. '*No.* You're too private. You would never want—'

'Okay, so maybe it won't be that big,' he conceded.

'But we need Adele and Bruno there, right? Definitely the coders and creatives.' He chuckled at her cringe. 'I need to prove to them I'm good enough for you.'

'You already are.' Despite her smile, Mia's eyes watered again. 'And your neighbours in Sicily.'

'We could marry there. Everyone could stay. Big party.' He stiffened slightly and cupped her face, looking directly into her eyes. 'Including Dario, if you want. I don't want to come between you and him. You only have each other—'

'You're not the one coming between me and Dario. It was our father who did that.'

'So invite him. I know you'd like to be closer to him.' He lowered his gaze. 'Family matters.'

'It does. He'll have to get used to you being mine.' She held him close.

'I'd like to build a big family with you,' he whispered.

'I would love that. Dogs, right?'

He laughed but his voice softened. 'And children. Three or four? Five or six? You pick.'

She giggled, too, and wriggled beneath him. 'You know I'm a little greedy.'

'And you know I love that about you.' He breathed in shakily. 'I'll try, Mia, but—'

'We'll make good lives for them,' she assured him. 'We'll never abandon them. We'll never make them feel…'

'Unwanted.' He rolled and pulled her to lie on his chest. 'We'll give them—'

'Love,' she breathed, adoring him with every fibre of her being. 'All our love.'

CHAPTER FOURTEEN

SANTE ARRIVED SLIGHTLY later than planned but he had good reason—one he couldn't wait to share with Mia. He ran up the stairs to fetch her, but stopped just in the doorway and blinked. The palazzo was full of people—cleaners, catering staff, florists—all being overseen by a very efficient, equally terrifying, wedding coordinator that Adele had hired. The older woman had become quite smug about her hand in their whirlwind romance.

I knew you'd be perfect for him, Mia.

She was, of course. But right now his perfect woman wasn't in sight. He snaffled a pastry from the pile on the counter, ignoring the combination of smiles and frowns the theft earned him, and backed out of the chaos and onto the balcony to look across the gardens as he quickly ate. A flash of colour clued him in. He went back to the car and carefully lifted out his precious cargo and walked towards the wrought iron summerhouse.

He heard her humming but couldn't see her from the back of the plush armchair. Carefully, he set the load down behind her and stepped around so she could see him.

'You found me.' She was curled up in one of the plush chairs.

'You knew I would.'

'I was just checking the place was ready for Dario and his fiancée.'

Her brother had accepted the wedding invitation they'd sent him a fortnight ago. Mia was nervously pleased about it. Sante was pleased she was pleased, but he didn't entirely trust that Dario wouldn't try to interfere. He was mentally rehearsing self-restraint—determined to stand alongside Mia should that happen. He wanted Mia to have everything. To marry him and still have a relationship with the brother she deeply cared about—even if things had been distant between them for a while. If Dario actually loved her, he would accept Sante's relationship with Mia for what it was. Genuine. All-encompassing, all-consuming love.

He hunched down before her. 'And got distracted? Needed a minute?'

'It's very busy in there even for me,' she said.

Sante had discovered that sometimes his effervescent, kind-to-everyone, sweet humming sunshine girl needed some space. She smiled but her eyes filled.

'Hey.' He cupped her face in both hands, frowning at the tears sparkling in her eyes. 'What's up?'

'I'm nervous,' she confessed. 'I don't want to have the night apart from you.'

Relief washed through him. 'I thought you said it's tradition,' he teased.

'Screw tradition. It was a stupid idea…' She bit her lip. 'Are you sure about this, Sante?'

Oh, his bride still didn't believe how much he loved her.

The past three weeks had been the best of his life.

They'd returned to Rome—to a party atmosphere in the office when they'd made the announcement. They'd taken the week off—gone to the concert, gone out to dinner, gone back to Sicily. He'd found her a ring and they were only just getting started.

'So sure,' he promised. 'You have my heart, Mia. Be gentle with it.'

'I'll hold it close and treasure it always.' Her smile went a little coy. 'Though I might not be as gentle with other parts...'

Chuckling, he leaned closer. 'I'll be with you tonight and every night that follows. I *never* want to be apart from you. I want you with me for the rest of my life. You're my anchor. My everything.'

Mia wrapped her arms around his neck and pulled him down to her. It was everything she'd needed to hear because the old insecurity was hard to overcome today. Sante could have *anyone*—yet he'd chosen her and she wasn't used to being wanted. Unbelievably—devastatingly—nor was he. But they would spend the rest of their lives loving each other. Completely.

'I can't wait for tomorrow,' he groaned. 'You'll be my *wife*.'

She loved that he shared his dreams with her. 'And you'll be my husband who right now tastes of—' She paused. 'Did you hear that?'

'What?'

'Scratching?' She wrinkled her nose. 'Oh no, do you think there are rodents in here?'

'No.' He smirked. 'I have a present for you.'

He drew her out of the chair and led her round to the oversize box sitting behind it.

'Are you going to unwrap it?' Sante prompted when she just stood staring at it.

Her heart raced because there was definitely something moving in there and she didn't want to guess in case she was wrong.

The paper was loose and lifted away at the first tear. It wasn't a box, but a wire crate and inside it was a floppy-eared, trembling-limbed puppy.

'Oh, Sante...' She dropped to her knees and drew the little darling out, her tears immediate and fast. 'He's *ours*?'

'Yes.' He crouched down with her, slinging a firm arm around her. 'He's ours. Always.'

Mia buried her face in the puppy's fur.

'I was going to research some dog breeders but there was an animal shelter not far from the airport and they'd just taken in a litter and—'

'And you rescued him.' She lifted her head and her heart swelled.

'Couldn't leave without him.' Sante shot her a sheepish grin. 'Figure we could start building our family right away.'

'Oh, yes. He's gorgeous.' She cuddled the puppy close, chuckling as it licked her jaw, when something dangling from the crate caught her eye. She reached for it and her laughter deepened. 'You got him a very blingy collar.'

'Actually, that's an extra little present in case you didn't like the dog—'

'How could anyone not adore this dog!' Then she shot him a look. 'You got a collar for *me*?'

'Look a little closer.' He winked.

She studied the tiny collar looped around the top rail

of the crate, gasped as she realised the 'bling' was actually a pair of sapphire-and-diamond drop earrings. 'Sante, they're stunning.'

'You don't have to wear them tomorrow. I just wanted to give you—'

'*Everything.* You've *already* given me everything.' She bent her head and breathed in the puppy's sweet scent again. 'They're beautiful and he's beautiful and you're *wonderful.*' She craned forward and pressed her mouth to his.

'Mmm.' He chuckled as she almost toppled over.

'Actually, I have a gift for you, too.' She had her present wrapped and hidden in here—it was the real reason she'd come in here before getting distracted by insecure thoughts.

He paused. 'You do?'

There was that hitch in his breath that she'd come to recognise—a hint of emotional vulnerability.

'It's hard to buy for a billionaire who could get himself whatever he wants, whenever he wants, but I thought of something. I think. Will you take him a minute?'

Sante took the wriggling bundle into his arms and cradled him close. Mia watched as the puppy sank against his chest and promptly fell asleep.

'He knows he's safe with you,' she whispered.

Sante looked at her and she fell in love with him all over again.

'Whereas he just wants to kiss you,' Sante chuckled softly. 'He and I have that desire in common.'

He carefully put the sleeping puppy back into the crate and tucked the blanket around him before turning back to her.

He unwrapped the present slowly, not tearing the paper the way Mia had, but taking care with it. Mia sat on her hands and refused to hurry him despite her nervousness. He was savouring the experience because it wasn't one he'd often had—a fact she intended to change.

The frame was facing down and she held her breath as he flipped it. He studied the black-and-white photograph she'd had printed for a long time. She was just about to ask when he cleared his throat.

'This is just before the concert and you insisted on a selfie.'

'To remember the moment, yeah,' she whispered.

'It's beautiful,' he muttered, still looking at it. '*You're* beautiful and we're...'

'Happy,' she said. 'I know it's just a selfie, but we're *us* in this and I thought it was time for you to have some family photos. We can have a house full of family photos. A house full of family.'

'There's nothing I'd like more. I love it. Thank you—' He kissed her.

But Mia broke away to giggle at a sudden, silly, *happy* thought. 'We'll need to have another taken with the puppy.'

'He can always be the ring bearer tomorrow,' Sante murmured through kisses.

'Oh, yes!' She laughed, joy bubbling up from a spring deep within that he'd filled. 'Oh, I love you, Sante.'

'And I adore you.' He bent his head to hers and pulled her into his strong arms. 'I always will.'

* * * * *

If you just couldn't get enough of
Enemies Until After Hours, *then be sure*
to check out the next instalment in the
Enemy Tycoons duet, coming soon!
And why not explore these other stories
by Natalie Anderson!

My One-Night Heir
Billion-Dollar Dating Game
Their Altar Arrangement
Boss's Baby Acquisition
Greek Vows Revisited

Available now!

Get up to 4 Free Books!

We'll send you 2 free books from each series you try
PLUS a free Mystery Gift.

FREE Value Over **$25**

Both the **Harlequin Presents** and **Harlequin Medical Romance** series feature exciting stories of passion and drama.

YES! Please send me 2 FREE novels from Harlequin Presents or Harlequin Medical Romance and my FREE gift (gift is worth about $10 retail). After receiving them, if I don't wish to receive any more books, I can return the shipping statement marked "cancel." If I don't cancel, I will receive 6 brand-new larger-print novels every month and be billed just $7.19 each in the U.S., or $7.99 each in Canada, or 4 brand-new Harlequin Medical Romance Larger-Print books every month and be billed just $7.19 each in the U.S. or $7.99 each in Canada, a savings of 20% off the cover price. It's quite a bargain! Shipping and handling is just 50¢ per book in the U.S. and $1.25 per book in Canada.* I understand that accepting the 2 free books and gift places me under no obligation to buy anything. I can always return a shipment and cancel at any time. The free books and gift are mine to keep no matter what I decide.

Choose one: ☐ **Harlequin Presents Larger-Print** (176/376 BPA G36Y) ☐ **Harlequin Medical Romance** (171/371 BPA G36Y) ☐ **Or Try Both!** (176/376 & 171/371 BPA G36Z)

Name (please print)

Address   Apt. #

City   State/Province   Zip/Postal Code

Email: Please check this box ☐ if you would like to receive newsletters and promotional emails from Harlequin Enterprises ULC and its affiliates. You can unsubscribe anytime.

Mail to the **Harlequin Reader Service:**
IN U.S.A.: P.O. Box 1341, Buffalo, NY 14240-8531
IN CANADA: P.O. Box 603, Fort Erie, Ontario L2A 5X3

Want to explore our other series or interested in ebooks? Visit www.ReaderService.com or call 1-800-873-8635.

*Terms and prices subject to change without notice. Prices do not include sales taxes, which will be charged (if applicable) based on your state or country of residence. Canadian residents will be charged applicable taxes. Offer not valid in Quebec. This offer is limited to one order per household. Books received may not be as shown. Not valid for current subscribers to the Harlequin Presents or Harlequin Medical Romance series. All orders subject to approval. Credit or debit balances in a customer's account(s) may be offset by any other outstanding balance owed by or to the customer. Please allow 4 to 6 weeks for delivery. Offer available while quantities last.

Your Privacy—Your information is being collected by Harlequin Enterprises ULC, operating as Harlequin Reader Service. For a complete summary of the information we collect, how we use this information and to whom it is disclosed, please visit our privacy notice located at https://corporate. harlequin.com/privacy-notice. Notice to California Residents – Under California law, you have specific rights to control and access your data. For more information on these rights and how to exercise them, visit https://corporate.harlequin.com/california-privacy. For additional information for residents of other U.S. states that provide their residents with certain rights with respect to personal data, visit https://corporate.harlequin.com/other-state-residents-privacy-rights/.

HPHM25